LOVE & FROST

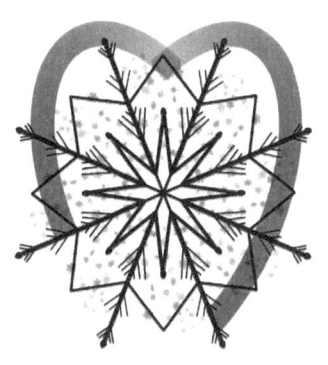

F. A. SENG

2024 Staton House Paperback Edition.

Love & Frost. Copyright © 2024 by F. A. Seng

faseng-author.com

All rights reserved.

The story, all names, characters, and incidents portrayed in this production are fictitious. No identification with actual persons (living or deceased), places, buildings, and products is intended or should be inferred.

ISBN: 979-8-89496-366-2 (paperback)

ISBN: 979-8-89496-370-9 (hardcover)

ISBN: 979-8-89496-364-8 (ebook)

Originally Published in 2024 in the United States of America.

TO MY LOVE,

SPENDING EVERY HOLIDAY WITH YOU MAKES IT ALL
BETTER.

You have my heart.

Phoenix
Rising
Press

'LOVE & FROST' PLAYLIST:

1. *'Last Christmas' by Wham!*

2. *'It's the Most Wonderful Time of the Year' by Andy Williams*

3. *'It's Beginning to Look a Lot Like Christmas' by Perry Como*

4. *'Underneath the Tree' by Kelly Clarkson*

5. *'We Need A Little Christmas' by Glee Cast*

6. *'Wonderful Christmastime' by Paul McCartney*

7. *'Where Are You Christmas' by Pentatonix*

8. *'The Christmas Song' by Nat King Cole*

9. *'Snowman' by Sia*

10. *'Happy Xmas (War Is Over)' by Christina Perri*

11. *'Have Yourself a Merry Little Christmas' by Michael Bublé*

12. *'New Year's Day (Taylor's Version)' by Taylor Swift*

13. *'I'll Be Home For Christmas' by Demi Lovato*

prologue

The cheers erupted around us, a deafening roar of celebration that felt like salt in an open wound. My heart thudded painfully against my ribs as Daniel's words echoed in my mind. It was early June, the warmth of the evening air heavy with the scent of blooming flowers, however, none of it seemed to matter anymore.

"I can't marry you. I'm sorry." He had said it so softly, so close to my ear, that it felt like a secret meant just for me.

I pulled back from our embrace, my hand slipping into my pocket to hide the ring box that now felt like a dead weight. My eyes locked onto his, searching his tired green eyes for something—anything—that would make this make sense. All I saw was sorrow etched deep into his face and the tears that streamed down his cheeks.

"W-what? W-why?" I stammer, my voice breaking as I try to hold onto him, my hands resting on his broad shoulders.

The Disneyland tank top he's wearing, the one that seemed so playful and light-hearted this morning, now only highlights the tension in his frame.

Daniel swallows hard, his gaze flickering everywhere except at me. We both know why, except I can't bring myself to face it. I'm not ready to let go.

"Is it because of yesterday's fight? If it is, we can work it out—"

His hand finds mine, the touch feeling foreign, like he's already drifting away. He guides me away from the crowd, leading me to a quieter corner near the entrance of Adventureland. The cheers and laughter fade into the background, leaving us in a bubble of silence that feels unbearably loud.

"It's been three years, Ethan," Daniel finally says, his voice barely above a whisper. "The fights haven't stopped. They've only gotten worse."

I drop my hands to my sides, anger and hurt boiling up inside me.

"That's ridiculous," I snap, the words spilling out before I can stop them. "You knew how important last month's client meeting was. I didn't cancel on your birthday by choice, I had to. I can't afford a Disneyland trip if I don't work when needed."

Regret gnaws at me the moment the words leave my mouth. I know how much Daniel has struggled, how his acting career has stalled with only a few Broadway shows here and there.

Still, I've crossed a line—if there's even a line left between us. Daniel laughs, it's a hollow, bitter sound that cuts through me.

"You did the same on my last birthday, our last anniversary; and the day my father died." His voice is raw, each word a punch to my gut. "It's always 'circumstances', Ethan. I'll never be your priority. What about me? My feelings? It's always work for you. You don't live in the present. It's all about the future and shit!"

His words hang between us, heavy and unyielding, until he speaks again, his voice quieter now and laced with hurt.

"And by the way, I landed a big production movie yesterday. It was supposed to be a surprise for you. That's why I planned dinner, but, of course, you didn't show up." He spits out as he turns away from me. I close my eyes, trying to keep the tears at bay.

"D-don't you love me?" I ask, my voice cracking with desperation. "The future is for us. I'm building it for us! I'd understand when you're at shoots. I'm not going to rake you over the coals for missing a date with me." My voice rises, anger mixing with the hurt, drawing a few glances from people passing by.

Daniel breathes out, shaking his head like he's finally done with me.

"Are you being serious, Ethan?" His voice is hushed. "Look, I do love you, it's just…" He hesitates, the words hanging heavy in the air. "It's not enough. Yes, I wanted to marry you except things have changed. You've just been with your work for a year. I need someone who's there for me. If you hadn't proposed today, I might not have realized it. It's clear now that we've reached a point where being right is more important than being together. Let's end this. Let's break up. I know you won't leave your work, so leave me."

one

A sharp smack on my head jolts me back. Jamie, my little sister, stands before me, unafraid and somewhat proud.

"You're zoning out again, Eth," she scolds, her playful hit making my coffee splatter on the windowsill.

The television plays a Christmas movie in the background, not the ad that just featured Daniel as an actor. His familiar face and voice pull me into a spiral of memories, yet Jamie's intervention snaps me out of it.

It feels as if Daniel's career skyrocketed within six months after our breakup.

This Christmas I thought I would be with Daniel and my family. After all, this Christmas would have been our third anniversary. I thought he would be my fiancé by now, instead, I'm here, sulking.

I stare out the window of our cozy dining hall, the scent of pine and cinnamon filling the air. I see snow blanketing Everest, a small town in Northern Michigan, transforming it into a serene, white wonderland. The old wooden houses line the streets, their gutters lined with heavy icicles.

"Do you mind? I was enjoying my existential crisis," I say, raising an eyebrow at her.

Jamie sighs, her black hair tied up in a bun. Her brown eyes glisten with concern as she chews her inner cheek. She looks a lot like me, with similar features— though I have high cheekbones and she's more on the chubby side. We're both carbon copies of our mom.

"You've been sulking since you got here. It's the holiday season, for crying out loud," Jamie says, her tone exasperated. "Aren't you a miserable soul without work? You've finally come home after years and look at you—" She rolls her eyes and I sigh, relieved she doesn't finish her sentence. It's been more than five years since I last celebrated Christmas with my family.

"Excuse me?" I walk toward the kitchen to set down my coffee. It's gone cold anyway. "I'm miserable? Really? You're the one smacking me like I'm a distracted student in your class. Aren't you the one missing work, missy?"

Jamie stands there, hands on her waist, eyes filled with disappointment.

"Besides…" I lick my lips, forcing a smile. "I'm meeting Tess and Brody in half an hour. Lots to catch up on!" I try to sound excited, but doubt creeps in, a familiar knot tightening in my stomach.

Will things still be the same with them? I'm not sure. I left Everest at eighteen on a full scholarship to New York University for marketing and the city's fast-paced life pulled me in. At first, I came home every few months, then once a year, and now only every five years.

I've changed, whereas this town feels frozen in time.

"You know I can see right through you, right?" Jamie's voice cuts through the silence, her tone piercing the fragile pretense I cling to. I turn away from her, pretending to focus on washing the coffee cup in my hands.

"Jamie, I'm fine," I say quickly, too quickly, my attention fixed on the soap suds swirling down the drain.

"Sure, you are," she replies, her voice heavy with sarcasm. "That's why seeing his face didn't bother you at all. That's why I found you drowning in vodka in your posh New York apartment. Thirty year-old Ethan still handles breakups like twenty year-old Ethan."

"Can you not—" I snap, annoyance flaring as I stare at the ceiling, trying to hold back the flood of emotions. Why did she drag me back here anyway? I hadn't planned on coming, but Jamie being Jamie had shown up at my apartment and practically forced me to come with her.

Why is she bringing up the past now?

"Eth, he's moved on," Jamie whispers, her voice softening with the empathy that makes her such a good teacher.

"Mm-hmm." I put the cup away and turn around, leaning my hands on the marble counter. "And I should care about him because?" I question, feigning obliviousness.

Jamie nods, not pressing further. "Just... be honest with yourself, Eth. That's all I'm saying."

"He broke up with me. Not the other way around," I say with a chuckle, though the sound feels empty in my throat. I force a smile, it's a shitty, fake smile at that. "I was out there building a life for us, except, of course, he didn't see that. Now, he's probably sucking some casting director's cock. Maybe that's why he turned down the engagement and put it all on me—to avoid the guilt."

The words hang in the air, weighted and bitter. Jamie gasps and only then do I fully grasp what I've just said. The venom in my voice lingers, tainting the space between us. Jamie's eyes widen, her expression a mix of shock and disappointment. I roll my eyes, bracing myself for the inevitable lecture about how much I've changed, how far I've strayed from who I used to be.

"You weren't like this, Eth." Her voice is low and laced with a sadness that pierces through my defensive walls. "You used to be caring and empathetic. What has the city done to you?"

A surge of anger flares inside me, hot and blinding. "It's called 'change', Jamie. You wouldn't understand because you've been stuck in this town for twenty-five years. Try moving out and broadening your horizons." The words come out sharp and cutting, a defense mechanism I don't even think to control. I see the hurt flash in her eyes and for a split second, regret washes over me. But I can't stop.

"You don't have to babysit me. I'm a grown man. I can do whatever the fuck I want. So stop trying to be the overbearing little sister and control every part of my life. I don't fucking need you to watch me all day every day."

Jamie's face tightens, the hurt now mingling with anger. Her mouth opens, the start of a sharp retort on her lips.

"Fuc—" she begins, but the sound of the front door swinging open cuts her off. Laughter and chatter fill the room as my parents walk in, arms loaded with shopping bags. Their voices carry the lightness of an afternoon spent together, oblivious to the shit storm that just passed between Jamie and I.

Jamie's face shifts, her hurt quickly masked by a bright, forced smile as she moves to help Mom with the bags. The tension lingers, a bitter aftertaste in the air that neither of us acknowledges.

"Did you two have fun?" Jamie asks cheerfully.

Dad comes over, clapping me on the shoulder and reaching for a bottle in the fridge. "That Collins guy! We went to his winter exhibition. Took ages. What an artist!"

"Collins guy?" I furrow my eyebrows as I notice Mom carrying a painting wrapped in bubble wrap. "Who even keeps an exhibition open this close to Christmas?"

Dad takes a swig of beer and starts unpacking shopping bags, while Mom carefully places the painting on the dining table. Jamie, now in her usual cheerful mood, joins in.

"You don't remember Collins? Jake Collins?" Jamie's surprise is evident as the painting slowly emerges from its protective wrapping. Bright reds, muted oranges, and yellows begin to reveal themselves.

"Jake Collins?" Recognition dawns on me and my eyes widen.

"The football player? The jock? He's an artist now?" I watch Jamie nod vigorously.

This town never ceases to amaze me. Jake Collins, who had once been the star football player and was headed to UCLA, is now a painter? That's hard to reconcile.

"Yes, yes," Jamie says with a playful smirk.

"Quite the handsome fellow, too." Mom smiles. Jamie raises an eyebrow and I feel my cheeks flush. High school crushes are long gone. Even so, I can't deny the pang of nostalgia.

Just then, the painting is fully revealed and I lean in, my eyes widening further.

The canvas depicts a serene scene in the small town of Everest. The small lake with a waterfall nestled in the fall foliage, the mountains draped in trees that shield the lake from view. It's a place I haven't thought about in years, a hidden gem only Jake and I knew.

"Such a lovely painting," Mom says, her voice filled with warmth. "He gifted it to us. He also remembers you, Jamie. And was happy to hear you're back in town, Ethan."

Jake remembers us and he gifted this painting to my parents? The connection isn't just a coincidence.

"That's interesting…" I whisper, my heart picking up speed.

My eyes stay glued to the painting, a small smile tugging at my lips as memories of quiet afternoons by the lake flood back. Those moments are vivid, like they just happened yesterday.

After school, Jake and I found refuge in that secluded spot by the lake. It wasn't planned; it was just a coincidence that we both ended up there after that forest party the summer before senior year.

LOVE & FROST

The day after that party, I started bringing my ukulele and sitting at the lake's edge, letting the stillness calm me as I practiced singing. Across the way, I'd see Jake working on his footwork, stones skittering with each precise kick. We rarely exchanged words, a silent understanding that this place was ours, except not together.

I tear my gaze away from the painting, the shock still settling in. "I had no idea Jake Collins had turned into an artist. Last I heard, he was all about football and UCLA."

Jamie shrugs, a teasing glint in her eye. "People change, Eth. Sometimes, they surprise us."

Mom chimes in, her voice excitable. "He's really made a name for himself."

I let my fingers drift over the canvas, feeling the raised texture of the brushstrokes. They're rough and deliberate, like they hold a story I'm only just beginning to understand.

"Did he say anything else?" I ask, aiming for casual, however, my voice betrays me with a flicker of curiosity.

"Not much," Mom replies, her attention already drifting, looking for a place to hang the new piece. "You might want to reach out to him. Gosh, it's been over twelve years since you graduated high school."

Time has slipped through my fingers like sand.

"I should," I murmur, the words more to myself than anyone else. "Maybe we could catch up."

"Absolutely." Jamie's eyes twinkle, a playful smirk dancing on her lips.

"What's that look for?" I ask, pulling my hand away from the painting as I glance at the clock. It's past eight already, Tess and Brody are expecting me.

Jamie just shrugs, her smirk deepening.

The tension between us from earlier seems to have dissolved, leaving behind a lightness between Jamie and I. We've always been pretty good about getting over our spats, which I've always loved, because I don't have the time to deal with silly fights and linger on them.

"I'm going to get ready and head out to meet my friends," I say to my parents, who are busy in a corner of the kitchen. They nod, smiling, before returning to their own conversation.

As I start up the stairs, Jamie's voice cuts through the air. "Ethan."

I stop, turning to look at her. "Yeah?"

"Are you really going to reach out to Jake?" she asks.

I shrug, "Maybe, why?"

Jamie's eyes light up and her grin widens, "Well, just so you know, Jake is into guys too."

My heart skips a beat, however, I force a casual tone. "And you're telling me this because…?"

She doesn't answer, just gives me that knowing smile that seems to hold a thousand unspoken words. I shake my head and walk upstairs to my room, letting out a long breath as soon as I'm alone.

Inside, my mind is a whirlwind and the only thing that keeps flashing through it is the countless times I listened to *"You Belong with Me"* by Taylor Swift, imagining myself and Jake together in some distant, impossible future. Jake Collins had been the golden boy of Everest High School.

Everybody liked him—teachers, students, even the janitor—and I was no exception. He was the guy who seemed to have it all: the looks, the charm, the way he moved through the world like it was all meant for him. From the way my parents talk about him, it feels like nothing has changed. Jake had been the golden boy then and he's still the golden boy now. Even after all these years, his shine hasn't faded.

Except I have changed.

I'm not the shy kid who used to like him from a distance. I've grown, I've lived a life far from Everest and I've built a confidence I never had back then.

two

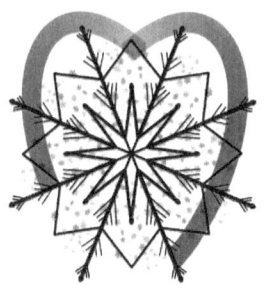

"Damn! Another promotion lined up? You must be working your ass off," Tess says, taking a sip of his beer. He looks so awestruck that I can't help but chuckle. "It's not that impressive," I reply, licking my lips and glancing around the place that used to be our go-to spot.

High Peak, a cozy little brewery café perched on a cliff, offers a stunning view of Everest below. It was Tess's father's place until he passed away a few years ago, leaving it to Tess. The Christmas lights twinkling around the town add a touch of magic, making everything feel quiet—so different from the bustling lights of New York City.

"Of course you'd say that," Brody remarks.

A man of few words, Brody can almost fade into the background if you're not paying attention. However, when he speaks, he never minces words. Straight to the point, with a touch of dry wit. "Everything's less impressive in the Big Apple."

I roll my eyes at his comment, but I smirk and lean back in my chair. "Well, some of us prefer climbing corporate ladders instead of just hammering nails into them, Brody," I shoot back, giving him a playful wink. "Hey, if I ever need a sturdy table to prop up my trophies, I'll give you a call."

Brody raises an eyebrow, a hint of a smile tugging at the corner of his lips. "Sure thing, Ethan. Just make sure those trophies aren't too heavy. Wouldn't want your high-and-mighty accomplishments to come crashing down."

I chuckle, shaking my head. "Don't worry, Brody. I've got confidence in your craftsmanship. If you can build a house, you can handle a few trophies."

Tess grins, jumping in. "You two are hilarious. Seriously, Ethan, when are you going to slow down and actually enjoy some of that success? I mean, the last time we all got together was five years ago. Maybe take a break? You're already a marketing director, right?" Tess leans forward, his elbows resting on the wooden table.

I shrug and nod. "I enjoy it just fine, Tess." I notice the pity in his eyes. He knows all about my history with Daniel. Tess has always been like a brother to me. Sure, we lost touch when Daniel came into my life and work got hectic, but if things had turned out differently, I would've wanted Tess as my best man.

We've kept in touch here and there—random texts, the occasional phone call, and the once-a-year visit if I could manage it. Still, it's nothing like before. With Brody, it's been even more sporadic. A couple of Facebook messages or quick updates about life and that's the extent of it. Everest has always felt like another world, a place I'd visit briefly before heading back to the rush of the city.

"Besides, someone has to keep up with the big city pace." I huff, pressing the matter a bit too much. "Not all of us can live the laid-back Everest life," I add, a subtle sting in my words, answering Tess's five-year remark.

I see the hurt flicker across his face and guilt twists in my gut. I hadn't meant to be harsh, however, they needed to understand why I couldn't stay in touch with them. I was busy.

"You were the one who stopped—" Brody starts. Before he can finish, a voice behind me cuts in.

"And what's wrong with the laid-back life?" The voice is raw and raspy, with a tone that drips with mockery. It's deep, familiar, and enough to send a shiver down my spine.

There's a sudden silence at the table, just the background hum of chatter and the faint strains of Andy

Williams' *"It's Beginning to Look a Lot Like Christmas"* waft through the air. It mingles with the smell of beer.

I chug the rest of my drink, frowning as I see Brody and Tess's eyes widen, their expressions shifting from surprise to something more like delight. "Nothing's wrong with it—" I begin, turning in my seat to face the person talking, except my words falter when I see him.

No, not just any guy.

A man.

Standing six feet tall, with the sharpest cheekbones I've ever seen. A smirk plays on his full, rosy lips, revealing a dimple on his left cheek. His silky brown hair, with a few gray tones, is perfectly styled, though one rebellious strand falls onto his forehead. The stubble on his face adds to his rugged charm.

For a moment, I can't place him—not until he removes the midnight blue Christmas scarf from his neck, revealing a tattoo—a simple triangle with a dandelion inside it.

My breath catches. "Jake Collins," I exhale, barely more than a whisper.

His smile broadens, crinkling the corners of his hazel eyes, which sparkle under the golden fairy lights strung across the ceiling. "Ethan Parker," he drawls, taking his time with my name. "Good to see you back in town. Looking to find your muse in the laid-back life again?" He winks and all I can do is stare, completely dumbfounded.

He's changed physically. He's more muscular now, his skin paler, despite that, it's still glowing under the subtle lights. He wears a forest green woolen jumper and cream pants, the loose fit hiding the toned body I can still imagine beneath. My heart skips a beat, memories of my high school crush flooding back. Jake Collins had been a star in my teenage years and now, standing before me, he's even more breathtaking than I remember.

"Christmas holidays," I swallow hard, suddenly aware of the tightness in my throat.

What is happening? I'm usually confident, but for some reason, my voice catches. I quickly regain my composure, letting a smirk curl at the edges of my lips. "Muse? Please, Collins. I don't need a laid-back life to find inspiration. I'm more into high stakes and bright lights these days," I reply, leaning in just enough to keep the banter alive.

"Touché," Jake replies with a throaty chuckle, his eyes locking onto mine with an intensity that makes my pulse quicken. The moment lingers, charged, until Brody clears his throat, snapping us back to reality.

"Jake… My boy! Have a seat. Did you bring what I asked you to?" Brody's voice breaks the spell and Jake nods, sliding into the empty seat across from me in our snug booth by the window.

"Yeah, it took a while to find the perfect match, nevertheless, I got it," Jake says, pulling a gift bag from beside him and handing it to Brody. Brody's eyes light up as he peeks inside, a genuine smile spreading across his usually stoic face. The sight piques my curiosity.

"What is it?" I ask, unable to mask the curiosity in my voice. My gaze flicks between Jake and Brody, waiting for an answer.

"His niece is visiting," Tess explains, filling in the gap when Brody remains focused on the gift. "She's really into books and Brody wanted to get her something special for Christmas."

"It's a vintage copy of *Pride and Prejudice*," Brody adds, finally looking up, his smile still firmly in place. "I knew Jake would be the one to help me find it. Thank you!" The charm in his voice is unmistakable.

"Anytime," Jake says with a smile and I blink in surprise. The last time I'd checked, Jake and Brody weren't exactly on friendly terms back in high school.

"What am I missing here?" I ask, raising an eyebrow. "I've been out of touch for five years, now I come back to find Jake and Brody acting like best friends." I chuckle, shaking my head at the irony. They had dated the same girl in high school, if I remember correctly—and things had been tense between them ever since.

Jake leans back in his chair, his smile softening as he glances at Brody. "Well, I moved back here from California three years ago and Brody was the one who helped me set up my art studio. He was the only one who agreed to take on the project." He pauses, a chuckle escaping as Brody nods. "Plus, we're older now. No point holding onto old grudges, right?"

I smirk, the memory of the painting Jake created coming to the forefront of my mind. "You do remember things," I say, locking eyes with him, hoping he'll catch the reference.

Jake holds my gaze, his expression shifting to one of quiet understanding. "I do," he replies, a small smile playing on his lips.

"What are your plans for Christmas?" Tess asks, waving over one of the staff to restock the beer pints and bring one for Jake as well.

Jake's smile tightens slightly as he replies, "Just me, myself, and I in the art studio." His tone is light, but something is off that makes me frown. A flicker of concern runs through me, however, I hesitate to pry. After all, we aren't exactly close enough for me to dig into his personal life, even though part of me really wants to.

Luckily, Brody steps in. "Is your mother okay now?" he asks, his expression growing more sympathetic.

Jake nods, the smile not quite reaching his eyes. "Yeah, she's doing better now." His tone is casual, but there's an underlying tension that doesn't go unnoticed. I watch as Brody and Tess exchange a knowing glance, leaving me feeling like the odd one out, the only person at the table who doesn't quite grasp what's going on.

If Jake is back in town, why isn't he staying with his family—especially during Christmas?

"Is your mom okay?" I ask lightly.

"Oh, yeah," Jake lets out an anxious laugh. "She's just been sick lately."

"Oh, I'm sorry to hear that," I say softly, placing a comforting hand on Jake's shoulder.

Tess claps his hands together, breaking the moment abruptly.

"Why don't you take Ethan with you to the studio for a bit?" Tess suggests, a mischievous twinkle in his eyes. "Give him a tour, show him how much this town has changed since he's been gone."

"He should what?" I sputter, nearly choking on my beer.

What the fuck?

Tess knows. He knows all about the ridiculous crush I had on Jake Collins back in high school. The one I thought I'd buried years ago. The last thing I need is Tess trying to play matchmaker when my life is already a tangled mess. A rebound isn't exactly on my Christmas list.

"Yeah, you should definitely see it," Tess continues, with a look on his face that makes me suspicious. "Jake's documented the entire town. It's really something. You should check out his winter exhibition. It's the last day."

So this was the exhibition where my parents got that painting.

"I mean—I—" I stammer, glancing at my watch. It's already eleven at night and my original plan involved nothing more exciting than heading home for a *Harry Potter* movie marathon. "I'm sure the gallery's closed by now. It's late."

"Actually, yes," Jake says, his voice carrying an inviting tone. "I've closed the gallery, but everything's still in place. I can take you there if you want to see it."

Before I can come up with an excuse or even agree, his phone buzzes. Jake steps away from the table to take the call, leaving me alone with Tess and Brody, who both look far too amused for my liking.

"What the hell, Tess? What was that?" I snap, turning to him, frustration bubbling up inside me.

Tess feigns innocence, a smirk tugging at his lips. "What was what?"

"Stop it. Why are you playing matchmaker? I'm not in the right state of mind for this. What the hell?" I try to keep my voice low even as the frustration seeps through. I let out a low sigh trying to calm my nerves which are making me feel, excited? "I appreciate what you guys are trying to do, but, for fuck sake, please don't meddle right now."

Tess just shrugs, but before he can say anything, Brody leans in, fixing me with a stern look. "Listen, Ethan," he says, his voice low and deliberate, the kind that makes you sit up and pay attention. "Your life is fucking black and white. You need some color. You need perspective."

I can't help the snort snort that follows, a mix of disbelief and irony. A straight guy telling me, a gay man, that I need more color in my life? We practically breathe colors. The seriousness in Brody's eyes makes me pause, the humor of the situation fading as I realize he isn't just talking about a palette.

"Perspective," I scoff, half-expecting Tess and Brody to crack up, however, their serious expressions don't budge. I sigh, realizing they aren't joking around.

"Fine. You both are coming too, right?" I ask, trying to keep the hope from creeping too obviously into my voice. The silence that follows isn't reassuring. "Right?"

They exchange glances, not saying a word and I feel a sinking feeling in my gut. Just as I open my mouth to protest, Jake slides back into the booth, his presence instantly shifting the mood.

"Sorry about that," Jake says, his tone casual, but his eyes are focused on me. "My assistant needed to confirm if she could take one of the paintings tomorrow." He pauses, letting the silence stretch for a beat. "So, you coming?"

I catch Tess and Brody's pointed looks from the corner of my eye. Before I can protest or make another excuse, I find myself nodding, my pulse quickening.

three

"We're getting pretty far from town," I mutter, a nervous chuckle escaping my lips. "Are you sure I'm not getting kidnapped?" I glance around, taking in the trees and scattered houses covered in snow. We're descending from the hill where Tess's café is, leaving the main city area of Everest behind. The further we go, the colder and more secluded it becomes. Even with the heater on full blast, the chill is creeping in through Jake's sedan.

"Ah, the classic kidnapping accusation," Jake replies, his eyes fixed on the road. As we pass under the occasional streetlamp, I catch the faintest hint of a smile playing at the corners of his mouth. The muted shine from the lights highlight the amusement in his eyes, making me feel a bit more at ease despite the eerie quiet of our surroundings.

"It's crazy," I chuckle, leaning against the window, watching the snowflakes drift lazily from the sky. "I was supposed to be in my room right now, cuddled up with my blanket, watching *Harry Potter*, but here I am."

"Are you complaining?" Jake asks, chewing a piece of gum that he just popped into his mouth and oddly, it feels very seductive, enough to make me look away and focus on the side mirror instead. The town, with its Christmas lights and cozy warmth, is fading behind us, leaving only the quiet, snow-covered landscape.

"What do you think?" I reply, a smirk tugging at the corners of my mouth. "Just so you know, Tess planned this. Sneaky fucker. They still think I have a crush on you."

Why the hell would I say that? The words slipped out before I could stop them. Now he's going to think that I'm some freak still obsessed over a silly high school crush.

"You have a crush on me?" Jake's voice holds a note of amusement and when I dare to glance at him, I see that he's grinning, his hazel eyes leaving the road just long enough to catch mine.

"Had," I correct quickly, feeling heat rise to my cheeks. "I had a crush on you. Past tense. Who didn't in high school?"

Jake's chuckle fills the car, rich and warm, I can't help but smile, even as I silently curse myself for letting that slip.

"I see," he says, not looking at me. I'm grateful for that.

As Jake's laughter fades, a comfortable silence settles between us, punctuated only by the crunch of tires on the snow-covered road. I glance out the window, watching as the town's lights disappear, giving way to an expanse of dark trees and deserted roads. The outside air looks colder, the kind of cold that seeps into your bones and lingers.

We continue down the road, which narrows as we approach the edge of town. The trees thin, revealing a frozen lake shimmering under the moonlight. A few abandoned properties stand in silhouette against the winter night, giving the area a hauntingly isolated feel. Yet, some houses are adorned with Christmas decorations, hinting at the presence of people.

"Why here?" I ask quietly, breaking the silence. "Why set up your studio so far out?"

"You'll see," Jake replies with a smile.

As we reach the end of the driveway, I see a small, one-story house decked out in glowing, incandescent lights along the roof's edge. The porch pillars are wrapped in lights and candy canes line the pathway leading up to the house.

It's charming—simple, yet endearing.

Jake parks the car and we step out into the brisk air. I shiver, the Burberry coat I'm wearing seems to not hold up against the cold, they're clearly made for fashion and not damn-near-freezing temperatures. My breath forms little clouds as I gaze out at the frozen lake, its surface unmoving and covered in ice and snow, bordered by a dense forest.

When I turn to face the opposite side of the lake, my jaw drops. The view is breathtaking.

"Now you know why here," Jake says, his voice warm against the chill as he pats my shoulder lightly. I can feel the faint heat of his hand through the thin fabric of my sweater and his minty breath brushes my ear. It's an electrifying sensation, but I keep my gaze fixed ahead.

Before me, Everest lays spread out like a winter wonderland. Tiny houses, each adorned with glowing Christmas lights. Paths are lined with festive decorations, casting a soft glow. In the distance, High Peak's roof stands out, bright with red and green lights.

"Why is this place abandoned?" I ask, glancing at the few empty properties scattered around. As Jake fumbles with the door lock.

The house next door is lit up with festive lights, suggesting it's still occupied. There are about eight houses in a neat row, each simple and charming. I rub my shoulders, missing the warmth that Jake's touch had provided.

"The weather's started to get rough with climate change," Jake explains as I turn to face him. "There are times when the power grid doesn't hold up here."

I notice a hand-painted banner beside the door.

The words 'Echoes of Everest' are crafted with stones, leaves, and flowers.

"Is this…" I start, trying to piece together its importance.

"Ah, my assistant Maria made the banner for the exhibition to welcome guests," Jake says. "She collected those materials from Everest itself and put it all together. It was sort of last minute because I was pretty behind on my work. Now, would you like to go in? Or would you rather stay out here with the cold?"

We both give a small chuckle as I nod, taking in the thoughtful details of the display and take a step inside.

The space is striking—its clean, modern lines and chic lighting creating a cozy ambiance. Paintings line the cream-colored walls, each piece bathed in a gentle, inviting glow. As I move from left to right, I let my eyes linger on each artwork, tracing the intricate details and the interplay of light and shadow. It feels like stepping into a new world with every painting.

"So, what kind of artist are you?" I ask, breaking the silence that's settled between us.

"The kind you want me to be," Jake replies, his voice light, but teasing. I raise my eyebrows in curiosity, glancing back at him as I continue into the gallery.

"What do you mean?" I ask, my fingers lightly grazing the edge of a frame as I shift my focus to Jake.

"Well, art is subjective and I work with many mediums," Jake says, his tone contemplative as he joins me by a particularly vivid piece. "I can't tell you what kind of artist I am. It's up to you to decide."

I study a painting that draws me in, its depiction of our old school rendered in an otherworldly shade of red, with the building itself washed in the colors of the sky—an inversion of reality. The intensity of the colors makes the scene feel both familiar and strange.

"And how do I decide that?" I ask, my voice barely above a whisper as I take in the surreal beauty of the painting.

Jake's breath is warm on the back of my neck as he replies, "By how I make you feel."

He stands close behind me, his hands neatly folded behind his back. I can sense his gaze on me, an unspoken connection forming between us as I absorb the painting's haunting allure.

"Why inverted?" I ask, my heart pounding as Jake's presence looms close. I can feel a shiver run down my neck and I shake my head, trying to focus. I close my eyes briefly, take a deep breath and turn to face him. "Why the inverted colors?"

Jake hesitates, his gaze dropping to the painting before he meets my eyes again. "Because the sky represents freedom, while school puts you in a box. Same schedule, same activities. Imagine a kid who wants to explore their own passions but is constrained to follow a predetermined path. In my world, I wanted the school to be the sky—an infinite space where anyone can pursue their true desires."

As he speaks, I'm drawn into his eyes, which convey a depth of emotion and understanding. "I don't think you understand—"

"I understand," I interrupt, my voice steady despite the rush of memories. "Out of all people, I understand. Being outed by someone at school, against my wishes, teaches you a lot about life."

The memory of that day still stings. I was fourteen, confused and awkward, when the boy I liked—a boy I trusted—outed me to everyone. We'd shared quiet conversations and moments that felt safe, but in one careless breath, he shattered it all. The whispers, the stares, the judgment hit me harder than I could've imagined. A wound that still has yet to heal; it's a reminder that trust can be fragile and easily broken.

I can feel the weight of it as I speak, the pain of that moment mingling with the empathy I feel for Jake's artistic vision.

"You get it," Jake says with a smile that softens his eyes. There's an unspoken apology in his gaze. "I remember how hard it was for you. We had just moved from Massachusetts. I just wanted to comfort you, but honestly, I was going through my own struggles of trying to fit in at a new school."

"Oh, please!" I wave it off, trying to lighten the mood. "You quickly became the golden boy of the school." His smile widens slightly and I can see the light back in his eyes.

I turn back to the painting of the school, trying to shift my focus. The image of the school, with its inverted colors, seems to pulse with a strange energy. I frown, lost in thought, as the painting's distorted reality clicks for me.

"Wait..." I say, my eyes narrowing as the realization hits me. "This painting isn't about the golden boy everyone knew. It's about the side of you that no one saw at school. This art side. All anyone knew was football."

"Bingo, Sherlock," Jake chuckles, his head falling back slightly. I watch as the gel he used to style his hair begins to lose its hold, revealing his natural curls. The transformation is striking—his curls frame his face with a softness that makes him look utterly captivating.

Before I can ask Jake about his shift from football to art, my phone vibrates in my pocket, making me curse under my breath. I excuse myself and answer the call.

"Where the hell are you?" Jamie's voice blasts through the receiver and I have to hold the phone away from my ear. I glance at Jake, who winces slightly at the volume.

"Calm down. I wasn't kidnapped," I say, giving Jake a sheepish smile. He mouths a grateful "I would never" while placing his hand over his heart.

"We were supposed to be coming up with interesting ways that Harry and Draco could get it in Hogwarts two hours ago. Where the hell are you?" Jamie's voice comes through again, more urgent this time. I look at my watch and see that it's already past 11:30 p.m.

"I'll be back in a little bit," I say quickly, hanging up before Jamie can say more. "I have to go," I say, stuffing my hands into my pockets.

"Yeah, I'll drop you," Jake replies, already heading for the door.

"You don't have to—" I quickly reply.

"Are you planning to walk?" Jake chuckles, I shake my head, a dismissive shrug escaping me. I climb into the car, grateful for the warmth and the unexpected company.

The drive is enveloped in silence, the quiet punctuated only by the hum of the engine and the crunch of tires on snow. The dim glow from the dashboard creates a warm cocoon inside the car, casting subtle shadows that dance across Jake's face.

Why does Jake's presence feel so oddly comforting?

As we cruise down the empty streets, I find myself stealing occasional glances at Jake. His profile, framed by the soft light, is both intriguing and calming. There's something magnetic about the way he focuses on the road, his eyes reflecting the occasional streetlight that passes by. Each time I look his way, I notice little things— the slight curve of his lips when he isn't speaking, the way his fingers rest casually on the steering wheel.

Soon, Jake pulls into my driveway, following the few directions I had given him. The car rolls to a stop and the engine's hum quiets to a muted purr.

"It's nice seeing you back in town," Jake murmurs as I unbuckle my seatbelt. I nod, feeling a sense of nostalgia.

"Yeah, it's a nice break from Manhattan," I say, shrugging slightly as I open the door.

"Why does it seem like you're pretending you don't like it here?" Jake's question takes me by surprise.

"What do you mean?" I ask, my tone sharper than I intend.

"The laid-back life comment," Jake says, recalling our conversation at High Peak. My mouth forms a small "O" as I realize what he means.

"Oh, that," I say, taking a deep breath. "It's true, isn't it? What is there here? It's like living in a bubble. The world outside is so different—you're missing out." I try to explain, my words feeling heavier than I expect.

"It's your home. That's what it is," Jake says slowly, his gaze steady. "How can you grow out of it?"

Jake's words linger in the cool night air, his tone slow and deliberate, as if he's genuinely trying to grasp why I distanced myself from home.

"I've built my own world in New York," I say, trying to hold onto my pride. "It took sacrifices."

Jake's eyes meet mine with an earnest intensity. "You know, Ethan," he begins, his voice hush, "Tess and Brody—whenever we all meet for drinks—they always talk about you. They share your stories and how proud they are of you. It just seems like you might be a little hard on them for choosing this life."

I'm taken aback. I hadn't expected Jake Collins to make me feel this pang of guilt tonight. I nod, speechless.

"I'll see you soon?" I ask, trying to shift the focus.

"Yeah," Jake smiles. "Do you want to give me your number and we can maybe find some time to hang out before you go back to the Big City?"

"I'd like that," I grin.

Jake hands me his phone, a smile playing on his lips. "Don't give me a fake number now," he laughs, his smile brightening as he watches me input my number.

With only two minutes to midnight, I hand him his phone, slip out of the car and walk to his window. "Thanks for the painting you gave my parents earlier today," I say, looking back at him. "I didn't think you'd remember that spot."

"Of course I do," Jake replies, his eyes twinkling. "I remember your ukulele practices. Still playing?"

I chuckle, a bittersweet smile on my face. "No, not anymore," I admit, a touch of sadness creeping in. I miss making music, but it's faded into the background of my busy life.

"Might want to dig it out," Jake suggests with a playful wink. "You played well."

I feel a blush creep up my cheeks as his gaze lingers. "Thanks, but I'm pretty sure it's been donated at this point, I haven't played since high school," I say softly.

"Damn, that's a shame," Jake says with care. "You were really good."

I smile up at him, not trying to make things awkward, "Well listen, thanks for dropping me off. Merry Christmas, Jake."

"Merry Christmas, Ethan," Jake replies, his grin wide and genuine.

As his sedan pulls away, I watch it disappear into the night, a smile tugging at my lips.

four

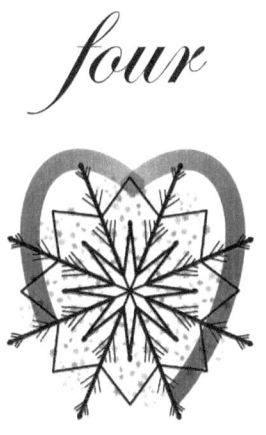

"Where the hell were you? And was that Jake who dropped you off?" Jamie's voice cuts through the cold air as she stands on the porch, wrapped in the baby blue onesie our parents gave her—our Christmas tradition. The sight of her waiting there, a mixture of worry and curiosity on her face, makes the chill seep deeper into my bones, even through the thick, navy Burberry coat I'm wearing. I don't answer right away, just brush past her and head inside, the warmth of the house wrapping around me like a blanket.

"He took me to his exhibition," I finally say, shrugging off my coat and hanging it up. I glance at Jamie, forcing a sarcastic smile. "Brody and Tess suggested it, so I went."

Jamie's expression shifts from confusion to surprise, her eyes searching mine for more. "I assume you had a good time?" she asks, following me as I head up the stairs. Her room is next to mine, our parents' room just down the hall near the living room.

"It was fine," I mutter, Jake's last words still echoing in my mind. They linger like an unwelcome guest, making me question if I've really been that guy— boasting about my new life to everyone, even to Jamie earlier.

"Okay," Jamie says, her tone sprinkled with disappointment as she turns to head into her room. I pause, guilt gnawing at me.

"Jamie, wait," I call out, moving toward her. Without thinking, I wrap her in a tight hug, pulling her close. I'd been a jerk to her earlier and I want her to know I'm sorry. She hugs me back just as tightly and when we pull apart, her face is a mix of puzzlement and concern.

"I'm sorry about earlier," I say, raising my hands in surrender. "I know you're just looking out for me."

A smile tugs at her lips and she playfully taps my head. "I'm glad you realized it. Good night, Eth," she says, sticking out her tongue in that familiar teasing way. "And by the way, I'm glad you're home this year."

"Me too," I reply in a whisper, watching her disappear into her room before I head into mine. What an eventful night it's been.

I close the door behind me and begin stripping off my clothes, the evening's events playing over in my mind. My phone buzzes, I glance at the screen to see a message from an unknown number.

Unknown Number:

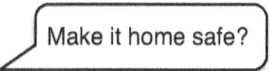

Make it home safe?

I can't help smiling as soon as I see the text. I know exactly who it is. Without hesitation, I save the number under Jake's name.

Me:

I should be asking you that. Did you make it home safe?

I set my phone aside and head into the bathroom to wash the day away, before I can fully enter, my phone dings with a new message. He must have replied right away. I sprint back to my phone before the screen can go dark again.

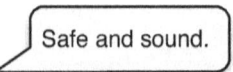

Jake:

> Safe and sound.

I let out a shaky breath until another message pops up from him.

Jake:

> I hope you liked the exhibition.

Honestly, I did enjoy the exhibition, but I've never been the artsy type. I'm more of a technical person, so I've always admired those with creativity—it's something I could never do.

Me:

> I really liked it, but as a corporate guy, I can't analyze it the way others might.

Jake:

> Wait, I never got to ask, how did my paintings make you feel?

I pause for a moment, thinking about how to put it into words before typing.

Me:

> Your paintings are beautiful, but it's more than that. They have character, I guess. Like the school one. It feels strange at first, but the longer you look at it, the more it pulls you in. It really sticks with you.

I bite my lip, watching Jake's name pop up as "typing," then disappear, only to start again. My heart races in anticipation until finally, the message comes through with a delicate ding.

Jake:

> Not bad for a corporate guy with spreadsheets. I'm impressed.

A smile tugs at the corners of my lips, growing wider as I read his words.

Me:

> You're cute.

Before I can process what I've just sent, I see it's already on its way. "What the hell, dumbass? That definitely wasn't meant to go out," I mutter.

Jake:

> Is this your way of flirting with me?

I stare at the screen, my mind racing. What had just happened? I blink, trying to process Jake's last message as I see him start typing again.

Jake:

> Anyway, you must have had a long day. Have a good night, Ethan.

I sit there, unsure how to respond. The words feel heavy in the silence of my room. I take a deep breath and type out a simple reply.

Me:

> Long, but worth it. Good night, Jake.

I switch off my phone and without bothering to change or freshen up, I collapse onto my bed. After a few moments of lying there with a silly grin on my face, the exhaustion from the day finally takes over and for the first time since the breakup, I fall asleep not thinking about what went wrong.

five

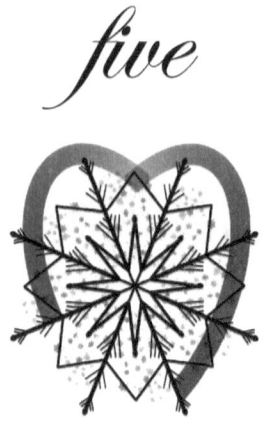

Before dinner the following day, we all sit back, basking in the warmth of the fireplace Mom has had on since she woke up.

"Oh. My. God!" Jamie punctuates, "Is that Ethan?!"

Mom and Dad howl with laughter, "Yes that is!"

"Oh, ew! Get that off the TV!" I shout, trying to get everyone to tear their eyes off of a six-year old me running around the house butt naked at Jamie's first birthday.

Suddenly, the doorbell rings, cutting through the laughter.

We all pause, exchanging curious glances. It's not like we're expecting anyone. Jamie shrugs and gets up to answer, her onesie flapping slightly as she moves.

I lean back in my chair, trying to ignore the flutter of anticipation in my chest. It could be a neighbor or just someone delivering late holiday wishes, but a part of me can't help but wonder if it's something—or someone—else.

"Ethan, someone's here for you!" Jamie's voice carries from the hallway, a teasing lilt to it that makes me instantly wary. She reappears in the living room with a sly grin, her eyes filling with mischief.

"Who is it?" I ask, pushing myself up from the couch. I take a few steps toward the door as Jamie just shrugs casually, turning her attention back to the old home videos playing on the TV.

The cool air nips at my skin as I step closer to the door. My heart starts pounding a little harder when I see who it is.

"Jake," I whisper.

He stands there, glancing at the neighborhood, a wrapped present in his hand. The black shirt and fur-lined coat hug his muscular frame, while his gray joggers add a casual touch to his otherwise polished look and as hard as it is to not stare, I can't stop from glancing down at the obvious outline of his dick. The snow has begun to cling to his hair, wetting the edges and making the gelled strands glisten under the porch light. His hazel eyes lock onto mine when he hears me whisper his name, the sight of him drop-dead gorgeous.

"Hi," Jake breathes out, his breath forming a small cloud in the cold air.

His lips, unexpectedly full and glistening in the winter chill, catch my attention, making me wonder how they manage to look so inviting despite the weather.

I take a step outside, closing the door softly behind me for some privacy. The crisp air wraps around us, but it does little to cool the heat creeping up my neck.

"What brings you here?" I ask, tilting my head slightly, trying to play it cool, even as my pulse quickens.

Jake shifts his weight from one foot to the other. His usual confidence seems to falter as he runs a hand through his damp hair, his fingers brushing against the snowflakes clinging to the strands.

"Uh…" He hesitates, his voice almost lost to the gentile hush of falling snow. "I was just… walking near the stores and I thought…" He pauses, his eyes widening slightly as he seems to lose his train of thought. "Never mind… Merry Christmas." His words tumble out and before I can respond, he thrusts the bag he's holding toward me, his cheeks flush with a faint pink from the cold—or maybe something else. "This… this is for you."

I blink, caught off guard by the uncharacteristic stutter in his voice. This is Jake Collins, the golden boy, the one who always seemed so sure of himself. Yet here he is, a little flustered, it's endearing.

"What?" I say, amusement threading through my words as I take the bag from his outstretched hand. "Thank you, but you didn't have to." I shake my head, still trying to wrap my mind around the fact that he'd gone out of his way to get me a gift.

"I know. I wanted to," he replies, his voice a little steadier now even though his gaze flickers away from mine, as if he isn't quite sure how I'll react.

I nod slowly, curiosity pulling at me as I peer inside the bag. It's heavier than I expected, the weight of it making me wonder what could possibly be inside. Jake's eyes follow my every movement, a hint of nervousness in them.

As I reach into the bag and feel the shape of the item inside, a rush of realization hits me. My heart skips a beat. No, he didn't… I pull the package out, my fingers trembling slightly with excitement and disbelief. The wrapping crinkles as I tear it open and there it is—a ukulele. A beautiful, sleek ukulele with a polished finish that gleams even in the dim light of the porch.

"Are you serious?" I finally manage to say, my voice barely above a whisper as I stare at it, completely stunned. "Why?"

Emotions surge inside me, a mix of gratitude, confusion, and something else I can't quite pinpoint. We barely know each other, not really—not beyond the superficial level. Yet here he is, standing in the cold, having gone out of his way to find something that holds a deeper meaning. Something that speaks to a part of me I hadn't thought about in years.

Jake's eyes soften as he looks at me and for a moment the world seems to narrow down to just the two of us, standing in the silence of a snowy winter afternoon.

"You loved it," he says, his voice gentle, almost as if he's afraid of breaking the moment. "And... I don't know, I just thought maybe it's something you'd like to have again. I want you to have it... Don't run away from things you love. They keep you sane during the worst times."

His words hit me in a place I didn't expect, a place I haven't really touched since I left home. Memories of lazy afternoons strumming the ukulele, the soft notes filling the air with a kind of joy I haven't felt in a long time, flash through my mind. The instrument had been a part of me, a piece of my identity that I'd somehow lost along the way.

"Jake, this is..." I struggle to find the right words, my throat tightening with emotion. "This is incredible. I... I don't know what to say."

"You don't have to say anything," he replies, a small smile playing on his lips. "I just hope you like it."

I glance down at the ukulele, its polished surface reflecting the dim porch light, then back up at Jake. For a moment, the cold, the snow, everything, fades away. It's just us and all the distance between us feels like it's vanished.

"I... I didn't get you anything," I finally admit, the words slipping out before I can stop them. An embarrassing feeling fills my chest and I feel like I'm coming up short.

Jake's lips curve into a gentle smile. "That's no worry. I just wanted to give it to you." He shrugs, trying to brush off the significance, but I can see the sincerity in his eyes. An awkward silence settles between us, the kind that makes the air feel thick.

Jake clears his throat, shifting his weight as if to break the tension. "Well, I'll take my leave then," he gives a small, silly salute. "See you around." He turns with a cute smile, starting toward his car, the snow crunching softly under his boots.

I watch him go, something in me resisting the idea of letting him just walk away. It doesn't feel right, not after the way he'd shown up here, not after the gift that carried so much meaning.

"Jake," I call out, my voice cutting through the quiet evening.

He pauses, a hand on the car door, and looks back at me. "Yeah?"

I hesitate, suddenly feeling the significance of the moment, but I can't let it pass. "It's been years since I went to the spot we used to hang out at after school. Do you… wanna go there tomorrow night, maybe?"

The question hangs in the air between us, tinged with a nervousness I haven't felt in a long time.

A grin spreads across Jake's face, making his dimples deepen and his eyes light up.

"I'll pick you up at five," he says, his voice warm.

I nod, watching him get into his car and pull away from the driveway. As the taillights disappear down the street, a realization consumes me like fire igniting dry wood. I've forgotten how much the small gestures matter and how they can bridge gaps you don't even realize had formed. In the chaos of my busy life, I've let go of the simplicity of enjoying the moment, of being present.

Here I am, back in my hometown, being reminded of that by the person who had once been my high school crush. It's like the universe is nudging me gently, but insistently, to remember what really matters.

"Why is Jake Collins gifting you something for Christmas?" Jamie's voice hits me as soon as I step back into the living room. The curiosity on my parents' faces mirrors her's and I suddenly feel like I'm under a spotlight.

I try to casually tuck the ukulele behind my back, except it's too late—they've already seen it.

"That was Jake at the door?" Dad asks, a note of concern in his voice. "You should have invited him in."

The way he says it makes me feel like I've committed some kind of social crime by leaving Jake out in the cold.

"Poor guy," Mom adds, her expression softening with sympathy. "His mom is really sick, you know? She's battling leukemia."

I blink, taken aback by the sudden turn of the conversation. "Wait, leukemia?" I choke. "Jake told me his mom was sick but didn't mention that it was cancer." Tears begin to fill my eyes. I can't imagine that pain he feels when he thinks about it.

Mom stands and covers me with one of her comforting hugs. "And the worst part of it all, his dad won't let him visit her."

"What? Why not?" I pull back slightly.

"His dad's not okay with Jake choosing art as a career," Jamie chimes in, her voice low. "And well... he's also kind of homophobic. That's why Jake lives alone in his studio."

"That's fucking bullshit," I mutter, the word barely escaping my lips. I can't wrap my head around it. Jake, with his easy smile and calm demeanor, is going through all of that and still, he'd shown up here with a gift for me.

"Yup," Jamie agrees, however, there's something else in the air, a tension that wasn't there before. I see the way my parents and Jamie exchange glances with something unspoken passing between them.

"What is it?" I ask, the uneasy feeling growing stronger.

Jamie hesitates and I can see the reluctance in her eyes as she finally speaks. "Daniel called to wish you a Merry Christmas."

I let out a long breath.

"He realized that you blocked his number so he tried the house phone," Jamie says quietly.

The name alone makes my heart clench. I don't want to hear it. The whole point of blocking him was to avoid moments like this and yet here it is, barreling toward me like a freight train.

"And?" I prompt, my voice betraying none of the turmoil brewing inside me.

"And… he's getting married," Jamie says softly, the words barely a whisper but landing with the force of a sledgehammer.

For a moment, I just stand there, the air thickening around me as the reality of it settles in. I can see my parents moving toward me, their concern clear, but I can't handle their pity right now. I can't handle any of it.

"I… I'm going to my room," I say, the words clipped short as I turn on my heel and walk away, shutting out the world behind me.

I know I can't blame Daniel for anything. He was right—I hadn't given him the time or attention he needed. If Jake's one small gesture could affect me so deeply, I can only imagine how my neglect must have felt to Daniel and knowing that doesn't make it any easier to accept that he's getting married so soon.

It feels like a punch to the gut, leaving me reeling with the reality that it's over.

For good.

I lie curled up in my bed, staring at the ceiling, lost in the void of my thoughts. My phone buzzes again on the nightstand, Jamie's name lighting up the screen for what must be the tenth time. I sigh, letting it ring. The weight in my chest refuses to budge, pulling me deeper into the mattress. I just don't have it in me to answer, not today.

"C'mon, Eth. Answer the damn phone," I mutter under my breath, knowing full well I won't.

Another buzz. Another missed call.

Instead, my mind drifts—back to a time when things were easier, lighter. Back to that perfect afternoon at the amusement park with Daniel. I can hear the laughter around me, the rush of the crowd, and Daniel's voice, teasing me as we stand in line for the Ferris wheel.

"Think we'll make it to the top without you freaking out?" Daniel smirks, nudging me with his elbow.

"Very funny," I shoot back, rolling my eyes. "I'm not the one who screamed like a little girl on the roller coaster."

Daniel laughs, that deep, rich sound that always makes me smile despite myself.

"You're never letting that go, are you?" He grins, shaking his head. "Fine. I'll take the Ferris wheel. As long as you're the one holding my hand when we're up there."

I smile now, the memory playing so vividly in my mind. I can still feel the warmth of Daniel's hand slipping into mine as the Ferris wheel lifts us higher, the city unfolding beneath us like a dream.

"You sure you're not scared?" Daniel whispers, leaning closer, his lips brushing against my ear.

I shiver, both from the height and the closeness. "Terrified," I reply, squeezing Daniel's hand tighter.

We sit in comfortable silence for a moment, the noise of the amusement park fading as we hover above it all. I look over at Daniel, my heart swelling at how relaxed he looks, his sunglasses perched atop his head, a rare grin stretching across his face.

"You look good," I say softly, almost to myself.

Daniel glances at me, one eyebrow raised. "Yeah?"

"Yeah." I smile. "This whole day—it's been perfect."

Daniel's grin softens into something more genuine, something that makes my heart skip a beat. "It's not over yet."

We step off the ride later, the sun dipping low in the sky, casting everything in a warm golden glow. A few people recognize Daniel, of course. It happens everywhere we go, the hushed whispers, the sideways glances and eventually, the brave ones who approach for a photo or an autograph.

"Hey, aren't you that guy from—oh my god, you're Daniel Morgan, right? From The Last Act?"

Daniel smiles politely, his grip tightening just slightly on my hand. "That's me. Thanks for watching."

The fan gushes, asking for a selfie, which Daniel obliges, all while keeping me close, never letting go of my hand. I try to play it cool, but inside, I'm glowing with pride.

"I'll never get used to that," I whisper once the fan leaves, grinning up at Daniel.

Daniel chuckles, pulling me closer. "You better, because I'm not going anywhere."

Later that evening, when the crowd thins and the lights from the rides blink softly in the background, Daniel leans in, his lips brushing against my neck, slow and deliberate. I shiver, my breath catching as I tilt my head, giving Daniel more access.

"Hmm, I could stay like this forever," Daniel murmurs, his voice low, his breath warm against my skin.

"You and me both," I whisper back, closing my eyes, feeling the world melt away around us.

My lips twitch into a small, bittersweet smile. The memory is so clear, so real, it hurts. I can still feel

Daniel's hand in mine, the way those lips felt against my skin, like I belonged to someone, to Daniel.

My phone buzzes again, pulling me back to the present. I don't move.

"Maybe I should've held on tighter," I whisper to myself, my voice barely audible in the quiet room. "Maybe..."

My phone buzzes again, lighting up with a message, this time from Tess. I groan, already knowing what it's going to say before I even check it. Another attempt to drag me out of my cave. Reluctantly, I pick up the phone and open the message.

Tess:

Hey, man. You free?

I stare at the screen for a second, already feeling a knot form in my stomach. Free? Sure, technically, I have nothing to do. But "free" doesn't really describe how I feel. The idea of socializing right now makes me want to crawl under the covers and disappear. I quickly type a reply.

Me:

Not really, man. Got some stuff to do.

It isn't the best excuse, however, I don't think I care too much. The last thing I want to do is explain why I don't feel like seeing anyone. Why the thought of sitting in a café and pretending everything is fine feels unbearable right now. I already canceled on Jake yesterday and feel pretty shitty for that, but the thought of seeing anyone when I'm still stuck on Daniel makes me feel even shittier.

I toss my phone onto the bed, roll onto my back and stare at the ceiling. The room feels suffocating, the air thick with the weight of all the things I'm not saying. My phone buzzes again. I don't move at first, but then curiosity gets the better of me and I reach for it.

Tess:

> You sure? Brody, Jake, and I are getting together for coffee and stuff. It'll be fun.

My chest tightens at the mention of Jake. Of course, Jake would be there. Tess always tries to pull us all together, like the old days, as if nothing has changed. As if I'm not completely unraveling inside. I sigh and type back.

Me:

> Nah, man. Really can't tonight. Another time, maybe.

Even as I hit send, I know I'm not being honest. It's not that I *can't* go—it's that I don't *want* to. I'm not ready to face them. Especially not Jake.

The phone buzzes again almost instantly.

Tess:

> You haven't been home in five years, Eth. C'mon, man, it'll be good for you.

Good for me? Tess doesn't get it. None of them do. How could they? They weren't the ones who had their heart torn out and stomped on. They aren't the ones lying here, rehashing every single moment that led up to the breakup, wondering where it all went wrong. I clench my jaw, glaring at the screen. Good for me? I barely even recognize myself anymore.

I throw the phone down onto the bed again and sit up, running my hands through my hair. The memory of Daniel is always there, lurking in the background, waiting to ambush me at any moment.

The phone buzzes again, but this time I ignore it. I know what Tess is trying to do and I appreciate it, I guess. No amount of coffee with the guys is going to fix this though. It's not going to stop me from replaying that last fight with Daniel over and over again in my head.

"It's been three years, Ethan. The fights haven't stopped. They've only gotten worse."
"The future is for us. I'm building it for us!"
"It's not enough."

Those words. I hate how they echo in my mind. *Not enough.* What does that even mean? I had been trying —working my ass off to make things better for us. I missed birthdays, sure. Anniversaries. It wasn't like I was out partying. I was working for us. For our future.

I scoff, standing up and pacing across the room.

Maybe I should've just gone. I think to myself, glancing over at the phone. Except what would that solve? Sitting around with Tess, Brody, and Jake wouldn't magically make things better.

I can picture the conversation already—Tess cracking jokes, Brody giving me that serious, understanding look, and Jake… Jake would ask me how I'm doing. He'd look at me with those calm, hazel eyes, I'd have to pretend that I'm not completely shattered inside. I'd have to pretend that Daniel's name isn't tattooed on every thought, every breath.

I shake my head, feeling the familiar bitterness creep back in. No. I'm not going. Not tonight. Not when everything still hurts this much. I'm not ready to face the world yet.

I walk back to the bed, picking up the phone one more time, the message still sitting there, waiting.

* * *

An hour later, a loud bang rattles the door, startling me out of my daze. I barely have time to process the noise before Jamie's voice pierces through the thin barrier.

"Ethan, open this door. Now."

I groan and bury my face deeper into the pillow, hoping she'll get the hint, but no. Jamie isn't the type to take a hint.

A second bang, even louder than the first. "I'm not leaving until you open up!" she hollers, her voice carrying that familiar edge of irritation.

"Go away, Jamie," I mumble, knowing full well she can't hear me, I'm just too drained to actually move. Another bang. God, she's relentless.

I reluctantly drag myself up from the bed, shuffling to the door. As soon as I crack it open, Jamie pushes her way inside, her eyes scanning the room like a detective at a crime scene.

She scrunches her nose at the mess of blankets on the floor and the half-empty water bottles littering the nightstand. "Seriously, Ethan? You're still in bed?" she snaps, hands on her hips. "It's been days. Get out."

"I'm fine, Jamie," I mutter, rubbing the back of my neck. "And it hasn't been *days*, it's been *a day*."

She ignores me, marching across the room and yanking the blankets off the bed. "You look like a zombie. You need to eat."

"I don't need to eat. I'm fine."

"Oh yeah?" Jamie's eyes flash with challenge. "You're so 'fine' that you've been hiding in this room most of the day yesterday and today, Mom's worried sick and I'm about five seconds away from dragging your ass out of here."

I sigh, knowing I have no fight left in me. "Fine. I'll get up."

She rolls her eyes but grabs my arm anyway, tugging me toward the door with more strength than I expect. "No. You're coming out now," she says firmly, pulling me down the stairs and into the kitchen. "Sit."

I sink into one of the wooden chairs at the kitchen table, my eyes trailing over the faint scratch marks on its surface from when we were kids. I haven't even realized how long it's been since I sat here.

Jamie spins on her heel, throwing open cabinets, pulling out bread, mayo, ham, and cheese. "You're eating. No arguments."

"I'm not hungry," I try, but she silences me with a glare that could melt steel.

"You're eating," she repeats, slapping a sandwich together and pushing it in front of me. "Now."

I stare at the plate, suddenly feeling five years old again. "This isn't necessary, Jamie."

"Oh, it's completely necessary," she shoots back, pulling up a chair across from me. "You can't just rot in your room. You look like you haven't showered in days. Have you even left the house?"

I grimace. "It's fine. I've just been... thinking."

Jamie lets out a frustrated huff. "Thinking. Right. About Daniel?"

I flinch. She knows. Of course, she knows. It's not like I can hide anything from her. "Maybe."

She folds her arms over her chest, leaning back in her chair. "And how's that working out for you?"

I don't answer. I don't need to. She can see the answer written all over my face.

After a moment of silence, she sighs and softens her tone. "Ethan, I get it. You're heartbroken. It sucks. Moping around like this? It's not helping. You need to get out of this house. You need to do something."

"I can't just—" I start, but she cuts me off.

"You can. You just won't," she says, raising an eyebrow. "Which, by the way, is ridiculous."

I pick up the sandwich, more to appease her than because I actually want to eat. I take a bite, chewing slowly, but it tastes like cardboard. "Tess invited me out tonight," I say between bites, figuring I might as well tell her.

Jamie's eyebrows shoot up. "Tess invited you out? With Brody and Jake?"

"Yeah," I mutter. "They're getting coffee at High Peak."

"You said no, didn't you?" she guesses, her expression already disapproving.

"I'm not in the mood for that right now," I say, pushing the plate away and slumping back in my chair.

"Not in the mood?" Jamie throws her hands up in exasperation. "Ethan, you haven't been in the mood for anything for weeks! This is exactly what you need—a chance to get out, see your friends, and remember that life doesn't revolve around Daniel."

I sigh, knowing she's right, but not willing to admit it. "It's not that simple, Jamie."

"Actually, it is," she says, leaning forward and giving me that determined look she always uses when she's about to lay down the law. "You can't just keep hiding from everyone. You need to talk to people. Be around people. Tess and Brody care about you. They've been asking about you for weeks. And Jake…" She pauses, raising an eyebrow. "You know, Jake's been back in town for a while now and you guys hung out the other day, why not get to know him a little better. You used to have a crush on him. Don't you think you might want to climb that tree?"

I roll my eyes, trying to dismiss the mention of Jake and the crush I had on him, but the truth is, the thought of seeing him again does make my heart race a little. "It's just… I don't know if I'm ready for all that."

"You're never going to feel ready," she says, her voice lowering. "That doesn't mean you should avoid it. You need this, Ethan. Sitting in here, reliving the breakup, it's not going to bring Daniel back. Your friends though? They'll remind you that there's more to your life than this."

I look at her, chewing my lip. She isn't wrong. I know I can't stay locked in this house forever, but going out and pretending like I'm okay when everything inside me still feels raw—it feels impossible.

Jamie reaches across the table and places her hand over mine. "Please. Just go tonight. Get out of here. See your friends. Let them in."

I stare at her hand for a moment, the warmth of her touch grounding me, pulling me out of the fog I've been lost in. "Okay," I mutter, my voice barely more than a whisper. "I'll go."

seven

The café door jingles as I step inside and the cozy atmosphere of High Peak immediately envelopes me, offering a sense of comfort. The smell of freshly brewed coffee and baked pastries fills the air, for a brief moment, I feel a sense of comfort. This place hasn't changed much since high school. I spot Tess and Brody at a table near the window, laughing about something.

Taking a deep breath, I walk over, trying to shake off the nerves buzzing under my skin.

"Hey, look who finally decided to show up!" Tess calls out with a grin, waving me over.

Brody gives me a nod, that quiet smile of his barely visible under his scruffy beard. "Glad you could make it," he says, standing up to give me a brief hug.

I pull up a chair, sinking into it as I force a smile. "Yeah."

"So," Tess leans forward, elbows resting on the table. "What dragged you out of your cave? Jamie lock you out or something?"

"Something like that," I say with a chuckle, though it comes out more awkward than I intended. "She pretty much forced me to come. Said I couldn't keep hiding out."

"Good for her," Tess says, giving me a pointed look. "You've been MIA for too long, Eth. We've been worried about you."

I shrug, not really wanting to get into it. "I saw you a few days ago."

"You know what I mean, Ethan," Tess says flatly.

The three of us are quiet for what feels like an eternity.

"So, where's Jake?" I ask, breaking the silence.

Tess and Brody exchange a glance. "He's running late, as usual," Brody says with a smirk. "Probably got caught up at the studio or something."

We start reminiscing about the old days—football games, school dances, the stupid pranks we used to pull on each other. Tess is midway through a story about the time he got detention for sneaking into the principal's office when the door jingles again.

I look up and there he is.

Jake Collins.

He walks in like he owns the place, wearing a black turtleneck and light gray jeans that cling to his lean, muscular frame. His dark hair is styled casually, a few strands falling into his face in that effortless way that makes him look like he's just stepped off a magazine cover. His eyes scan the café until they land on me and he smiles.

"Hey, sorry I'm late," Jake says, making his way over to the table. "Lost track of time."

Tess waves it off and laughs. "No worries, man. You're always late."

Jake leans back in his chair, setting one of his arms around me as he looks at the others. "What've I missed?"

"Just talking about high school," Brody says with a chuckle. "The good old days when you were the golden boy on the football field."

Jake laughs, a deep, rich sound that sends a shiver down my spine. "God, that feels like a lifetime ago."

"I still can't believe it," I chime in, glancing over at him. "You went from football to art. What inspired the switch?"

Jake's smile softens and he shrugs. "Yeah, well... people change. I loved football, don't get me wrong. After high school, it just didn't feel the same. I guess I wanted something more... creative."

"Creative," Tess snorts. "You make it sound so deep. You were always sketching in the back of class when you should've been taking notes."

Jake rolls his eyes. "Okay, maybe I wasn't as dedicated as I should've been in high school, but hey, it worked out."

I find myself smiling despite the nervous energy still thrumming through me. It's weird, sitting here with Jake after all these years, talking like we used to. At the same time, it feels kind of… right. Like no time has passed.

"You remember that last game?" Brody says, leaning forward. "The championship? Jake scored the winning touchdown and the whole school went nuts. You were like a god back then."

Jake shakes his head, chuckling. "Man, that game… I haven't thought about it in ages. It was insane, though. The crowd, the pressure… but yeah, it was a good day."

"I think half the school had a crush on you after that," Tess teases, nudging him with a grin. "Not that they didn't already."

Jake smirks, as his eyes flicker over to me for a second and I feel my face heat up. "I wasn't paying attention to all that," he says, waving it off.

Trying to break the tension, I quote one of the best movies of all time, "So you agree? You think you're really pretty?"

Jake lets out a loud cackle, "Okay, Gretchen."

I crane my neck quickly and dramatically to look directly at Jake, "I think you mean Regina."

Jake smiles over at me, "Same thing, I mean, come on, who has watched that movie in the last ten years?"

My jaw hit the floor in shock. "I'll have you know, I watch it multiple times a year because it's such a classic."

He laughs a deep, contagious laugh. "Maybe we can watch it together someday."

"Oh, we definitely will," I smile and Jake laughs softly.

Tess and Brody's eyes go wide and watch Jake and I go back and forth with huge smiles on their faces.

Jake shrugs again, leaning back in his chair, his arm still comfortably resting over the back of my chair. "Life's funny like that. You think you know where you're headed and then—bam—something changes and you end up somewhere completely different."

I nod, understanding that feeling all too well. "Yeah, I get that."

Tess raises his coffee cup in a mock toast. "To change, then. God knows we've all been through plenty of it."

We all clink our cups together and as I take a sip of my coffee, I can't help but glance at Jake, his hand slowly sliding to my upper back. A gentle spark spreads through me, the simple touch grounding me in a way that makes everything feel more certain, more real. Things have changed, sure. But sitting here with them, with him, I realize maybe that's not such a bad thing.

We chat for a while, the conversation easy and light, filled with jokes and stories from our teenage years. I'm starting to feel a little more like myself, a little more grounded. Jake's arm stays around my shoulder for most of it, his warmth making the evening a bit easier to get through. It's surprising how comfortable it all feels—like the years haven't created this massive gap between us.

Brody stretches, checking his watch. "Alright, I gotta head out. Got a meeting with an investor in about an hour."

Tess raises an eyebrow. "Investor? For what?"

"Yeah, seriously," I chime in, smirking. "Who's investing in carpentry? What, are people betting on your next table being a bestseller?"

Brody chuckles, shaking his head. "You're not as funny as you think, Parker." He grabs his coat, standing up from the table. "The world's changing, man. People are into handmade, custom stuff now. They want quality, not mass-produced crap."

Tess nods in agreement. "It's true. People are all about that artisan vibe these days."

I'm still skeptical. "Okay, but investors? For furniture?"

Brody looks at me, a devious shimmer in his eye. "Not just furniture. I've started making a few art pieces on the side. Sculptures, wood carvings. After seeing Jake's stuff, I was inspired."

My jaw drops and I blink at him. "Wait... what? You're doing art now too?"

Brody shrugs like it's not a big deal, but there's pride in his voice. "Yeah, I mean, I've always been good with my hands, right? Decided to try something new. Turns out people like it. Apparently a few of them even want to invest in what I'm doing."

I stare at him, genuinely shocked. "You're kidding."

"Nope," Brody replies, crossing his arms. "Got a couple of orders lined up already. Some rich folk love the idea of one-of-a-kind pieces in their fancy homes."

Tess leans back in his chair, grinning like a proud parent. "Told you it would work, didn't I?"

I glance between them, still trying to process the idea of Brody, the guy who used to nail together makeshift skate ramps, now creating art pieces that investors want to back. "I'm honestly shocked. Never in my lifetime did I think I'd see you doing art. But hey, good for you, dude."

Brody shrugs again, pulling his phone out of his pocket and reading a text message. "Like I said, the world's changing. People appreciate craftsmanship. Anyway, I gotta jet. Catch you guys later."

He gives a quick wave and makes his way out of the café, leaving the three of us sitting there in a moment of stunned silence. Tess chuckles to himself, shaking his head.

"You should see some of Brody's stuff," he says, turning to me. "He's actually really good. Not that I ever doubted it, but still, it's impressive."

I shake my head, still in disbelief. "Brody, the quiet guy who could barely draw a stick figure in art class, is now making sculptures. The world really has changed."

"Speaking of change," Tess says, standing up from the table, "I need to run some errands for the café. Orders and all that. You guys good?"

"Yeah, we're fine," I say, glancing over at Jake. "Right?"

Jake flashes me a small smile, his arm slipping from my shoulders as he leans forward, resting his elbows on the table. "Yeah, we're good."

Tess gives us a curious look, something like amusement playing at the corners of his lips. "Alright then. I'll catch you guys later." He tosses his apron over his shoulder and heads out the back door, leaving me and Jake sitting there, alone.

I shift in my seat, suddenly hyper-aware of how quiet the café has become. My fingers drum nervously on the table. "So, uh… what should we do now?"

Jake leans back in his chair, stretching out his legs. "We could just hang here if you want. Or…" he says before trailing off.

"Or?" I ask, raising an eyebrow, genuinely curious as to what he had in mind.

"We could just go for a walk," he suggests, his tone casual. "You know, take a break from sitting around. Clear our heads."

A walk. It sounds simple enough and honestly, the idea of getting outside, away from the walls that seem to close in on me every time I think about Daniel, isn't a bad one. Maybe some fresh air will help take my mind off everything—at least for a little while.

"Yeah," I nod. "A walk sounds good."

* * *

As Jake and I stroll along the tranquil street, I'm surprised at how easy it is to fall into conversation with him. It's not like we have much to talk about—just random things, little stories, and bits of banter. It still feels… natural. A lot more natural than I thought it would, especially after all these years.

We walk past a few shops, the dim glow of their lights reflecting on the wet pavement. That's when I notice the small, cozy bookstore on the corner. Its windows are fogged up from the warmth inside and through the glass, I can see rows of old wooden shelves packed with books of every size and color.

Jake nudges me with his elbow. "Hey, you see that place?"

"Yeah," I say, glancing at him. "Looks kinda cool."

Jake grins. "Let's check it out."

I raise an eyebrow. "You're into books now too?"

He chuckles. "Always have been. This place is great—they've got some really interesting stuff. Come on."

We push open the door and a small bell chimes softly as we step inside. The bookstore's inviting heat greets us instantly, surrounding us like stepping into summer after a chilly swim. The familiar scent of old paper and leather wafts through the air, a welcome sensation. The cozy atmosphere is undeniable, with mismatched armchairs nestled into quiet reading corners and the gentle hum of jazz playing in the background.

Behind the counter a young woman looks up from the book she's reading and smiles. "Hey, Jake!" she says, waving casually.

I turn to Jake, raising an eyebrow. "You come here often?"

He shrugs, that easy smile still on his face. "Yeah, I guess you could say that. I like places like this. Feels… inspiring. Plus, they've got some great books on art and design. It's kind of a hidden gem."

I nod, glancing around. The store definitely has that indie charm, with books crammed onto every available surface, old lamps giving off a golden hue and handwritten notes stuck to shelves offering recommendations. It feels like the kind of place you could lose yourself in for hours.

Jake wanders over to one of the shelves, his fingers grazing the spines of the books. "I found a lot of my favorite art books here," he says, more to himself than to me. "You never know what you'll find."

I follow him, picking up a book at random. The title is something like *The Art of Japanese Ink Painting.* Not exactly my thing, but Jake seems to light up as he scans the shelves.

"You know," I say, "I'm still wrapping my head around the fact that you're this… artsy guy now. Like, the Jake I remember from high school? Total football star. Now you're all about books and art. It's weird."

Jake smirks, pulling out a book and flipping through its pages. "Yeah, well, people change. High school Jake wasn't exactly the deepest guy, you know?"

"I guess none of us were," I say with a smile, picking up another book. "I barely recognized Brody with his whole art thing either."

Jake nods. "Right? It's wild. You'd never think either of us would be into that and that's why life's full of surprises."

We meander through the store for a while, neither of us in a rush to leave. There's something relaxing about just being here in this serene space filled with stories and ideas. I haven't felt this calm in a long time.

Jake suddenly stops in his tracks, his eyes scanning one of the bookshelves. "Hey, you know what?"

"What?" I ask, leaning against the shelf beside him.

"We should get a map of the town," he says, like it's the most obvious thing in the world.

"A map?" I raise an eyebrow. "What for?"

"Why not?" Jake grins. "We're walking around anyway. Let's see if we can figure out a cool route—maybe check out some spots we haven't seen in a while."

I blink at him, then giggle. "A map? Like we're tourists?"

"Exactly like we're tourists," he says, looking way too excited for what sounds like a pretty basic idea.

I shrug, amused. "Alright. Sure. Let's do it."

Jake walks over to the counter, where the receptionist is still buried in her book. "Hey, do you guys have a map of Everest?" he asks.

She looks up, her eyes brightening when she sees him again. "Yeah, we've got a few. One sec." She reaches under the counter and pulls out a folded map, handing it to him with a smile. "Here you go. We don't get a lot of requests for these, but they're handy."

"Thanks," Jake says, unfolding the map right there on the counter.

I lean over, peering at the slightly faded map of the city. It's detailed, with little markers for landmarks, cafés, shops, and parks.

Jake's eyes scan the map thoughtfully. "Let's find somewhere interesting," he says, dragging a finger across the paper.

I snort. "We've lived here for years. What? Suddenly you don't know the layout?"

Jake shoots me a look. "You'd be surprised. I haven't been everywhere."

We find a quiet corner of the bookstore, tucked away from the rest of the space and sit down at one of the little tables by the window. Jake spreads the map out between us, his expression a mix of concentration and excitement, like we're about to embark on some grand adventure.

"Okay," he says, pointing to a spot near the river. "We could head down here. There's this cool new art installation near the park. Or we could swing by the old neighborhood. See if anything's changed."

I lean back in my chair with my arms crossed, watching him with a smirk. "This is like the most random thing you've ever suggested."

Jake shrugs, grinning. "You said you wanted to do something. So here we are, making a plan."

I can't help but laugh. "Alright, fine. Let's do it. Don't expect me to be impressed by an art installation."

Jake chuckles, folding up the map with a dramatic flourish. "We'll see about that."

I smile, grateful for the distraction. "Lead the way, then, Mr. Tour Guide."

* * *

Jake and I wander through the streets, map in hand, with no real plan except to see where the night takes us. After a while, we find ourselves walking down a familiar road—the one that leads to our old high school.

As we turn the corner, there it is, standing just as we left it all those years ago. The large, two-story, brick building, built in the early 2000's, looms in front of us, the playground across the street still bustling with kids even though the sun has already dipped behind the trees.

Jake stops, staring at the school with a small smile on his face. "Man, this place. It feels like a lifetime ago, huh?"

I chuckle, stuffing my hands into my jacket pockets. "Tell me about it. Seems like nothing's changed."

We stand there for a moment, watching the kids run around the field, laughing and playing tag just like I did as a kid. The sound of their carefree joy stirs up a lot of memories, ones I haven't thought about in years.

"Remember when you used to watch me play football over there?" Jake nods toward the field. "You were always the guy cheering us on like we were in the NFL."

I laugh, shaking my head. "Okay, hold on," I start. "I wasn't just watching you." *Yes I was.*

Jake grins, nudging me with his shoulder. "Riiight."

"I wasn't!" I insist, a smirk tugging at my lips. "Even if I was, would that really be so bad?"

Jake rolls his eyes, but he's still smiling. "No, I would've loved it. I did love it."

We walk closer to the field, watching the kids playing. One of them trips and falls and before we can react, he hops back up and keeps running like nothing happened.

"That used to be me," Jake says softly, his eyes distant as he watches the scene unfold.

"Yeah," I agree. "Again, another lifetime."

Jake smiles wistfully, his hands shoved in his pockets. "We spent so much time out here. Football games, hanging out after school…"

I nod, the memories flooding back. "I remember I used to try get you to sneak out of practice early sometimes. Hit the old café near the square before anyone noticed."

Jake chuckles. "I forgot about that. Coach was always so pissed at you for that."

"Yeah, well, I had priorities," I say, grinning. "I mean, I *did* have a crush on you."

We stand there for a few more minutes, just taking it all in. The school, the memories, the feeling of being young and careless. It's weird being back, like stepping into a time capsule. I hadn't realized how much I missed it until we were standing here.

Finally, Jake glances over at me. "You ready to keep moving? We've got more places to see."

I nod, taking one last look at the field before turning away. "Yeah, let's go."

We wander through the streets until we reach the town square. The moment we step into it, the energy hits me. The square is bustling with life—vendors line the streets, selling everything from fruits to handmade crafts and the air is filled with the sounds of people talking, giggling, and haggling over prices. It feels like a completely different world from the child-filled football we just left.

Jake's eyes light up as he looks around. "I forgot how lively it gets here at night. It's like a mini-festival every evening."

I nod, scanning the scene. "Yeah, it's kind of cool. Everyone seems so… happy."

We stroll past the stalls, taking in the sights and sounds. There are vendors selling brightly colored scarves, handmade jewelry, wooden toys, and all sorts of knick-knacks. One stall is packed with fresh fruits and vegetables, the smell of ripe strawberries making my mouth water. Another has trinkets hanging from the awning—charms, beads, and small tokens people can buy for luck or protection.

Jake suddenly stops in front of one of the stalls, eyeing something hanging from a string. It's a small charm, made of a black feather and a ring carved from a seashell, simple but somehow striking.

"Hey, check this out," he says, pointing at the charm.

I lean in for a closer look. "What is it?"

"It's a lucky charm," the vendor chimes in with a thick accent, smiling at us. "The feather is for protection and the ring is to bring good fortune."

Jake studies it for a second, then smiles and turns to the vendor. "How much?"

"Five bucks," the vendor says, holding it up for Jake to inspect.

Jake hands over the money without a second thought and the vendor passes him the charm. Without hesitating, Jake turns and holds it out to me. "Here. For you."

I blink, surprised. "Wait, what? Why?"

He shrugs, that easygoing grin still on his face. "Just because. Call it a 'welcome back to life' gift."

I stare at him, then at the charm in his hand. It's such a simple gesture, but for some reason, it hits me harder than I expect. After spending so much time feeling like I'm stuck in this endless loop of memories about Daniel, this small thing—this little token—feels like a way out. A reminder that there's still more to life than what I've lost.

I smile, reaching out to take the charm from him. "Thanks, I… I appreciate it."

Jake smiles, that warm, genuine kind of smile that makes me feel like maybe everything isn't as hopeless as it seems. "No problem. You could use a little good luck."

I snicker softly, holding the charm in my hand and studying it. The black feather feels soft under my fingers and the seashell ring glimmers faintly in the evening light. "Yeah, I think I could."

We walk around the square a bit longer, taking in the sights and sounds of the bustling crowd, except my mind keeps drifting back to that small charm in my pocket and how, in a way, it feels like a turning point. I'm not sure where things are headed from here, but for the first time in a long time, I don't feel completely lost.

As we walk toward the edge of the square, I glance at Jake. "So, what now?"

He grins, looking down at the map he's still holding. "I think we let the map decide."

I laugh, shaking my head. "Alright, lead the way, Mr. Tour Guide. Let's see where this map takes us."

eight

I'm lounging in my living room, strumming the ukulele Jake gifted me. The quiet, cheerful notes fill the air, a perfect soundtrack for the holiday spirit swirling around me. I glance at the decorations—twinkling lights and colorful ornaments adorning the tree. It finally feels like Christmas.

"Ethan! Dinner's ready!" my mom calls from the kitchen, the scent of roasted turkey and spices wafting through the house.

"Coming!" I reply, setting the ukulele down and joining the rest of the family at the dining table. My dad is already there, carving the turkey, a look of concentration on his face.

"Don't take too much. We need room for dessert," my mom jokes, placing a steaming bowl of mashed potatoes beside him.

"Who could say no to your cooking?" Dad chuckles, dishing out generous servings for everyone.

After the delicious meal, we gather around the tree, ready to open presents.

"Ethan! Taylor Swift Era's tour tickets? Are you kidding me?" Jamie's eyes widen as she tears open her present. They're in my company's VIP box. Her voice cracks with disbelief and I see tears well up almost instantly.

"You've always wanted to go, right? Plus, it makes up for the five Christmases I've missed," I say, shrugging nonchalantly.

Jamie doesn't need another invitation. She launches herself at me, hugging me tightly, her gratitude spilling over as she peppers my face with kisses. I push her away playfully, laughing.

"Ew! Get off me," I say, grinning as our parents chuckle from the couch.

I glance over at Mom and notice a tear slipping down her cheek. Her gaze is fixed on us, her phone clicking away to capture the moment. Jamie and I groan in unison, knowing those photos will soon become her Facebook profile picture.

Home.

The word echoes in my mind as I watch Jamie's beaming face and the joy radiating from my parents. Jake's words about never outgrowing home feel true at this moment. Seeing my family so happy is a comforting reminder of where I truly belong.

"You're different today," Jamie says, giving me a sidelong glance as we watch our parents unwrap their gifts. "Something's up."

"It's Christmas," I deflect, more focused on our parents' reactions.

"A trip to Spain?" Mom's voice wavers with disbelief as she holds up the envelope.

I grin. "Yes. You both deserve a vacation. When was the last time you got out of town?"

"You're really spoiling us, Ethan and Jamie! This is incredible," Dad says, his face lighting up with a broad smile. The tears in his eyes make it clear he's more than happy and I can feel the importance of the moment fill my heart, the kind of feeling Jake always talks about.

Jamie and I have planned this gift for months. We know how much they've always dreamed of traveling and now that we can afford it, this Christmas feels like the perfect time. Dad's work in real estate means he can adjust his schedule and Mom, who spends most of her time at home, needs a change of scenery more than anyone. The appreciation and love on their faces is the real gift.

Jamie claps her hands excitedly, her eyes sparkling. "Now it's time for you to open my gift!"

I roll my eyes and a grin spreads across my face as I carefully unwrap the box. Inside, nestled in tissue paper, is a limited-edition Marvel comic I've been eyeing for months. My grin stretches wide and I glance at Jamie, who is already beaming.

"Thanks, Jamie. This is awesome."

She rolls her eyes, pretending to brush off the praise, but I know she's pleased.

Next, I unwrap my parent's gifts. The classic red jumper Mom knitted for me is soft and slightly itchy, yet it's still a comforting reminder of home. Dad, knowing my obsession, has gotten me the anime book set I've been coveting. The thoughtfulness behind each gift makes my heart swell.

As we chat about the gifts and dinner my phone buzzes on the table. I glance down to see a text from Jake.

Jake:

> Hey! Can we go out again tomorrow?

I can't help but smile, my heart racing a little. "Um, guys, give me a second," I say as I type out a quick reply.

> Yes! I'd love to! Can't wait!

I hit send, a big grin spreading across my face. Just as I turn back to the family, my mom asks, "Who was that?"

"Just Jake," I reply, unable to hide my excitement.

"Oh, the cute one?" she teases, wiggling her eyebrows. "You two are becoming quite the pair, huh?"

"Mom!" I exclaim, my cheeks warming. "We're just friends, hanging out!"

She laughs and my dad adds, "Just friends, huh? I remember when I said that about your mom."

"Okay, okay, let's not get into that," I groan, but I can't help smiling. The thought of spending more time with Jake tomorrow has me feeling all kinds of happy.

nine

I walk into the café, the warm air enveloping me like a hug. The smell of fresh coffee and baked goods is irresistible. As I scan the room, I spot Jake at a corner table, his face lit up by the sparkle of the fairy lights strung above.

"Hey! Over here!" he calls, waving me over.

"Hey there!" I reply, sliding into the seat across from him. "Ready to plan our next adventure?"

"Absolutely!" Jake grins, his enthusiasm infectious. "So, what do you have in mind?"

I pull out my phone, scrolling through a few ideas. "I was thinking we could check out that new art exhibit at the gallery downtown. I heard it's amazing."

"Sounds great! I've been wanting to go there, but first, let's grab something to drink so we can warm up. It's freezing outside!" he says, rubbing his hands together as he glances out the window at the swirling snow.

I nod in agreement. "Definitely! I'll get us some hot chocolates."

After a quick trip to the counter, I return with our drinks, steaming mugs in hand. "Cheers to creativity and warm beverages!" I say, clinking my mug against his.

"Cheers!" Jake laughs, taking a sip. "So, after the gallery, what do you think? We could check out a local bar? I hear they have amazing cocktails."

"Good idea! We could use a little celebration after all this planning," I say, my excitement bubbling over.

As we sip our drinks, the temperature outside drops and the wind howls against the windows. I shiver a little. "Wow, it's really getting chilly. I didn't realize how cold it was until now."

Jake looks thoughtful for a moment. "You know, we could just go to my art studio instead. I have a few jackets there and we can stay out of the cold for a while."

"Your art studio? That sounds perfect!" I say, feeling a surge of anticipation. "I've always wanted to see where you create your magic."

"Okay, then it's settled! Let's finish up here and head over," he says, his eyes sparkling.

We finish our drinks, laughing and making jokes about our clumsiness in the snow. As we step outside, the biting wind hits us like a wall.

"Ugh! I should've worn more layers," I joke, pulling my scarf tighter around my neck.

Jake chuckles. "Yeah, I definitely underestimated the weather. But don't worry; I've got you covered—literally!"

As we make our way to his studio, I can feel myself getting pulled deeper into the conversation, pushing back the chill. I'm eager to see Jake's world, his art, and everything that comes with it.

"Just wait until you see my latest piece," he says as we walk. "I think you'll really like it."

"I can't wait! I'm sure it's incredible," I reply, genuinely excited.

We arrive at his studio and he pushes the door open, revealing a cozy space filled with canvases, brushes, and splashes of color everywhere. "Welcome to my second home," he says, a hint of pride in his voice.

"It's amazing!" I exclaim, stepping inside. "I love the vibe here."

"Make yourself at home," Jake says, grabbing a couple of jackets from a nearby rack. "Let's get you warmed up."

As he hands me a jacket, our fingers brush and I feel a jolt of electricity between us. I can't help but smile as I slip it on. "Thanks, Jake. This is perfect."

While Jake rummages through the clothes, I lean against the wall, admiring the art around me. "You have such an incredible collection here," I say, gesturing to a colorful canvas that catches my eye. "Is this one of your pieces?"

"Yeah, that one's from last summer. I was inspired by the beach," Jake replies, pulling out a navy jacket. "What do you think of this one?"

"Perfect! It matches your eyes," I tease and he shoots me a playful glare.

"Flattery will get you everywhere, Ethan," he says, grinning as he tosses me a deep green blanket. Just then, the wind outside begins to howl, making the studio shudder.

"Wow, that sounds intense. Is it really getting worse out there?" I ask, glancing at the window. The snow is coming down harder now, swirling around like a blizzard.

"Let me check," Jake says, walking over to the window. He pulls the curtain aside and a gust of wind rushes in, causing him to stumble back. "Whoa! That's definitely a storm."

My phone buzzes, lighting up the screen. I glance down to see a hazard warning flashing across the screen: **Severe Weather Alert: Stay Indoors.** "Uh, Jake? We might be stuck here for a while," I say, feeling a twinge of concern.

"Great. Just what we need," Jake mutters, rushing to the doors and windows. "Can you help me close everything?"

"Of course!" I smile.

We scramble around the studio, pushing windows shut and locking doors. Just as we secure the last window, the lights flicker and then go out completely.

"Jake?" I call, suddenly engulfed in darkness.

"I'm here," he replies, his voice steady, but with an undercurrent of nervousness. "Just stay where you are. I'll find a flashlight."

I take a cautious step forward, my foot catching on something on the floor. "Whoa!" I stumble, reaching out for something to steady myself.

"Ethan, are you okay?" Jake's voice is closer now.

"Yeah, just tripped over… something," I say, trying to navigate in the dark. I can hear him moving toward me and soon enough, our fingers brush against each other in the dark.

"I've got you," he says softly, I feel a sense of security at his touch. "I told you not to move." I can hear his smile through his words.

The lights flicker back on, only for a moment, just long enough to reveal our intertwined fingers. I pull my hand away, my cheeks flushing with embarrassment. A second later, the lights went back out. "Uh, wow. That didn't last long."

Jake chuckles, his cheeks a shade pinker. "Yeah, definitely not how I pictured our evening going. But, hey, at least we're not outside in that storm."

He pulls out his phone, the hazy glow of the flashlight casting a dim circle of light around us. I follow suit, fumbling for mine, and the two beams cut through the darkness, illuminating the small space.

"True," I say, trying to shake off the awkwardness. "I'm glad we're together. I mean, it could be worse, right?"

"Exactly! Plus, I've got art supplies and hot chocolate!" Jake grins, clearly trying to lighten the mood. "We can have our own little storm party. Let's clean up a bit before we begin." Jake pulls out a towel and throws it over his shoulder. "I'm going to grab a quick shower. The storm's not going anywhere, so make yourself comfortable."

I watch him disappear toward the bathroom, feeling a little flustered. The winds outside are rattling the windows violently and I settle onto the couch, waiting for Jake to return. The studio feels cozy despite the storm raging outside.

When Jake steps back into the room, it's quicker than I expect. His voice breaks through the quiet. "I have a feeling the power's going to be out for a while. This storm's no joke."

I glance up and the sight nearly takes my breath away. Jake stands there, freshly showered, with a towel draped around his neck. His torso glistens under the dim light of the studio, muscles accentuated by the gentile light. His joggers hang low on his hips, just barely staying in place. The casual, effortless way he carries himself makes it impossible to look away.

Every time Jake moves, the subtle shift of the towel or the play of light on his skin makes my pulse quicken. Despite my best efforts, I'm completely captivated. I try to keep my breathing steady, except the way he brushes a hand through his damp hair, the casual confidence in his movements—it's all too much.

Jake stretches, reaching for a nearby canvas and the sight of his body moving so fluidly intensifies the tension in the room. The storm outside rages on, but inside the studio, a different kind of storm is brewing between us. When Jake turns to glance at me, a teasing smile playing on his lips, I know this moment is teetering on the edge of something intense.

"You want to paint something?" Jake asks, his voice breaking the charged silence as he approaches me. His footsteps are slow and deliberate, causing a knot to form in my stomach. I turn to look out the window, where the storm outside has turned the world into a swirling mass of snow and wind. The warmth of the studio feels even more inviting now, but I need a moment to collect myself before the tension overwhelms me.

I wander over to the window, noticing the single bed positioned nearby. Above it hangs a painting of a dandelion, its delicate details far more intricate than the minimalist tattoo on Jake's neck.

"You like dandelions?" I ask, my curiosity getting the better of me. As I turn to face him, I find Jake has slipped into a plain white t-shirt, now speckled with paint. I let out a breath I didn't realize I was holding.

"My sister, Holly, likes them," he says, his gaze steady. My brow furrows. As far as I know, he's an only child.

I glance around the studio, taking in the raw brick texture of the wall next to the bed. It's adorned with photo frames, each one a window into different moments of his life—childhood memories, football practice, prom with a queen by his side, and scenes from his Californian days.

"I thought you were an only child," I say, turning back to Jake. His eyes follow my every movement, his expression unreadable.

"No, she's my half-sister. Lives with her mother, Maria, in the Philippines. Maria cut ties with my dad when I was ten. I never got a chance to say goodbye to Holly. I got the tattoo as a memory," Jake explains, his voice steady, but laced with underlying sadness. This is a side of him I haven't seen before.

"Wow," I murmur, processing the new information. "You don't know where she is now?"

"No," Jake says simply. "Actually, you're the first person I've talked about this with."

My eyes go wide. "Oh, come on. You must have told someone about the tattoo."

Jake shrugs, his casual demeanor almost too nonchalant. "I've never had a partner; never someone I felt close to enough to tell."

I stare at him, incredulous. "What? That's not possible. You're thirty."

Jake chuckles softly as he walks toward a wooden shelf in the corner, stacked with papers, colors, drawing books, and assorted stationery. His back muscles ripple with each movement and I try to focus on something else, but it's impossible.

"You don't believe me?" Jake asks, a playful edge in his voice as he reaches for a canvas on the top shelf.

"No, it's just… hard to believe," I admit, my voice betraying the admiration I feel as I watch him move with a fluid grace. He grabs a canvas, his movements effortlessly confident. I try to keep my focus on the work he's doing, except the sight of him in that simple white t-shirt, with paint stains creating an abstract pattern, is almost mesmerizing. "Plus, you dated girls in the past."

Jake glances up, a smirk playing at his lips.

"Those don't count. They were just teenage flings." He continues setting up the easel, each motion deliberate and precise. "I prefer being on my own. It's like being a free spirit. The idea of getting my heart broken and then painting about it—it would just ruin my art."

I let out a low chuckle, shaking my head.

"That doesn't make sense. Art is supposed to be a way to express and release your personal experiences."

Jake shrugs, a nonchalant smile on his face.

"Not necessarily. But yes, I've had my share of dating and well, you know... I'm not exactly a saint."

I almost choke on my breath at his matter-of-fact tone. "Right."

Jake's gaze shifts to meet mine directly, a curious spark in his eyes. "What about you?"

I glance around the studio, feeling the weight of his question. I pick up a Rubik's cube from the side table, its surface adorned with creative patterns, a reflection of Jake's artistic touch. I twirl it in my hands, studying its intricate designs, before settling onto the edge of the bed.

"Well, let's just say I've always prioritized stability," I begin, my voice fading a bit. "I've been in relationships before. In fact, I got stood up at Disneyland about six months ago. I was too focused on work and he felt like I wasn't really there for him. He ended up turning down my proposal."

"Ouch," Jake says, his voice carrying a sympathetic edge. He pauses, a thoughtful expression crossing his face.

"But…" I prompt, sensing there's more he wants to say.

"But he's not entirely wrong," Jake says, his attention still on the canvas. He dips a brush into a palette of colors, thinning them with practiced ease. "From what I've heard, you do seem to prioritize your work. You just exist. You're not living."

I stand up from the bed and move closer to him, watching as he works. The studio is filled with the tender rustle of his brush strokes and the faint scent of paint. Jake's focus is intense, yet there's a subtle ease in his movements.

"You don't even know me," I say, standing beside him and peering over his shoulder.

Jake glances at me, his eyes holding a steady gaze.

"I know you enough." He hands me the palette and brush with casual confidence. "As I said, your friends talk a lot about you."

"But that's not me," I say, my voice quiet yet firm. "That's their version of me from five years ago."

"Then show me who you are now. The present version," Jake says, his voice low, however, his words hold a gentle command.

He reaches out and takes my hand, guiding it toward the canvas. A sudden breath catches in my throat as his fingers lightly graze mine, the sudden feel of his touch sending a shiver through me. The proximity is electrifying; his body pressed close to mine, his scent—an intoxicating mix of paint and something undeniably Jake—fills my senses.

With deliberate motion, Jake moves my hand up and down, the brush strokes translating into vivid red streaks on the canvas. The red paint flows across the canvas, creating bold, expressive marks that seem to capture something raw and real.

I'm acutely aware of the way Jake's body presses against mine. The heat from his skin seeps through the thin fabric of his shirt, creating a comforting bubble around us. His chest is solid against my back, the rhythmic rise and fall of his breathing mirrors mine, creating an intimate cadence that feels almost like fate.

Jake's fingers, guiding mine across the canvas are firm, but gentle, sending tingles up my arm.

His breath is warm against my ear as he speaks softly, "Let the paint show you who you truly are now. Not who they think you were."

Just as I'm about to respond, my phone buzzes. I glance at the screen and see that it's Jamie. I hesitate for a moment, unsure if I should answer. I don't want to interrupt this moment with Jake. After the third ring,

Jake laughs. "You should probably get that before she files a missing person's report."

Jake and I both cackle hysterically.

I swipe my finger on my phone to answer the call. "Yes, Jamie. I'm safe. I'm at Jake's art studio," I say, trying to dismiss the concern in her voice. It's past midnight and the storm has intensified. The wind howls outside, rattling the windows and the snow falls in a relentless fury. The forecast predicts it won't clear until morning, with the worst of it expected in the early hours. I know staying put is the safest option and Jake, ever the gracious host, has assured me I'm welcome to stay.

"Jake, huh?" Jamie's voice carries a teasing tone, I can practically see the sly smile on her face. I fight to keep my expression neutral, not wanting to give her any ammunition. Jake is only a few feet away, seated at his desk near the opposite window, completely absorbed in his sketchbook. The gentle radiance of the lamp illuminates his face, casting shadows that accentuate the sharp angles of his jaw and the focused intensity in his eyes.

He looks like he belongs in that moment, surrounded by his art, his expression one of quiet concentration as he sketches. The way his hand moves fluidly across the page, the way he occasionally pauses to study his work before continuing, is mesmerizing.

"Yes, I'll be careful. Tell Mom and Dad not to worry. I'll head out in the morning," I say, ending the call with Jamie. I can almost see her nodding through the phone before the line goes dead. With a sigh, I get up from the bed and walk over to the canvas I've just finished.

It's far from perfect, but it's mine—free from the rigid rows and columns of spreadsheets that dominate my daily life.

"You should frame it and take it to your office in Manhattan," comes Jake's deep, raspy voice from behind me. I turn to find him leaning back in his office chair, his body relaxed, his gaze steady on me. The thin frames of his glasses perched on his nose are a new addition and they somehow make him even more attractive, lending an intellectual edge to his rugged charm.

"It wouldn't fit with the aesthetics over there," I reply, a small smile playing on my lips. "The office is plain, boring. Everything is sterile—white walls, gray desks. This," I gesture to the painting, "would stick out like a sore thumb."

Jake doesn't say anything right away, he just watches me with those piercing eyes of his.

"It might be just what the place needs," he finally says, his voice low.

"Do you really think so?" I ask, stepping closer to where Jake is sitting, his sketchbook still open on the desk. My eyes wander over the array of sketches and notes scattered across the wooden surface. It's clear he's deep into planning something intricate.

"What's this?" I ask, tilting my head to get a better look.

Jake turns his chair slightly, his gaze following mine. "The winter festival," he explains. "I'm organizing an exhibition. Friends from all over the country are coming to showcase their work. I can't afford any mistakes."

"Wow," I say, memories of the festival flooding back. "I almost forgot we still have those. I used to love going."

"I do remember those times as well," Jake replies.

It's around 3a.m. when the clouds begin to clear and the wind dies down. We talk a bit more, but the tiredness takes us both out in a single sweep.

ten

I wake up to a bright, blinding light pouring in through the curtains. I blink a few times, rubbing the sleep from my eyes. As I sit up and peer out the window, the world outside is blanketed in a thick layer of fresh snow. The street looks like something out of a winter postcard—everything plush, white, and untouched.

Kids are already out there, bundled up in puffy coats and scarves, running around, throwing snowballs, and rolling up snowmen. I smile at the sound of their laughter echoing through the quiet morning, giving the neighborhood a lively buzz.

I look down and realize that I'm still at Jake's. I must have fallen asleep in his bed after we spent the night reminiscing about old times and catching up on everything new. I also notice I'm still wearing a pajama set he lent me and My mouth lifts in a quiet smile at the lingering scent of him on the fabric. I may have basked in the scent a few times too many.

Turning to look at Jake, who's still fast asleep beside me with his arm lazily draped over my waist, I can't help but think of how comfortable he makes me. Stifling a laugh, I carefully slide out from under his arm. He looks so peaceful, like he's hibernating. But I'm starving and the thought of breakfast sounds too good to resist.

I pad over to the kitchen and flip on the light switch. To my delight, the power seemed to have turned back on sometime last night. I begin quietly rummaging through the fridge. "Eggs, bacon... perfect," I mutter to myself, gathering what I need. As I crack the eggs into the pan, I decide it's probably a good time to check in with my parents.

Grabbing my phone, I dial my mom's number. She picks up almost immediately.

"Ethan! Are you okay? We heard about the storm!" she exclaims, her voice full of concern.

"Yeah, Mom, I'm fine. No need to worry," I say, trying to reassure her. "The snowstorm wasn't as bad as it seemed. We're all safe and warm inside."

"I'm so glad to hear that," she sighs with relief. "Is Jake there with you?"

"Yeah, he's still asleep. I'm making breakfast," I reply, flipping the bacon in the pan.

"Well, make sure he knows he's always welcome at our house for the holidays," she adds, her tone softening. "You know we'd love to have him."

"I know, Mom. We'll see you soon. I promise," I say, smiling at the thought. "I'll call you later, okay? Love you."

"Love you too, honey," she says before hanging up.

I put the phone down and glance out the window again. The kids are now in the middle of building an enormous snowman. I chuckle, watching them struggle to lift the middle section. As I stir the eggs, an idea suddenly strikes me.

A grin spreads across my face. *Why should they have all the fun?* I think to myself.

I quickly plate the breakfast, leaving some on the counter for when Jake wakes up and pull on my jacket and boots. Quietly, I open the door, stepping out into the icy morning air. The snow crunches beneath my feet as I make my way over to the kids.

"Hey! Need a hand with that snowman?" I call out to the group of children.

They look up, surprised to see me, but their faces quickly brighten. "Yeah! It's so heavy!" one of the boys exclaims, his arms raised in exasperation.

I chuckle and kneel beside them. "Alright, let's do this together. On the count of three, we'll lift it up. Ready?"

They nod eagerly and I count, "One, two, three!" Together we hoist the middle part of the snowman onto the base. "Perfect! Now, how about we make this guy really special?" I suggest grabbing some sticks for arms and an old scarf from the porch.

The kids giggle as we finish the snowman, adding a carrot nose from one of their homes and a crooked hat I found inside. One of the girls claps her hands. "He looks awesome!"

"He does," I agree, brushing the snow off my gloves. "You guys did a great job."

I stand outside Jake's studio, my breath visible in the frigid air, my hands tucked behind my back, hiding the freshly, loosely-packed snowball. A mischievous grin spreads across my face as I dial his number.

The phone rings a few times before I hear a groggy, familiar voice on the other end. "Hello?"

"Good morning, sleepyhead," I say, barely able to suppress my laughter.

"Ethan? What time is it?" Jake mumbles, clearly still half-asleep.

"Oh, just time for some fun! Listen, I'm outside your studio. Do me a favor and open the front window, would you?"

"What? Outside? Why?" Jake's voice is full of confusion, but I can hear him shuffling out of bed.

"Trust me. You'll see. Just open the window," I urge, my excitement bubbling over.

"Alright, alright," he says with a yawn, his footsteps growing louder as he moves toward the window. "You better not be up to something."

"Me? Never," I lie, the smirk growing wider on my face.

The window creaks open and Jake sticks his head out, his hair a mess and his eyes squinting against the bright snow. "What's going on?" he asks, rubbing the back of his neck.

I can barely hold in my laughter as I see him standing there, still not fully awake. "Close your eyes," I say sweetly. "I've got a surprise for you."

Jake gives me a skeptical look, but a smile tugs at his lips. "Okay, fine. What is it?" He closes his eyes, his smile widening.

"Keep them closed… and no peeking!" I say, trying to contain my excitement.

"No peeking," Jake confirms, his voice playful now. "What's the gift? Should I be worried?"

"Not at all," I say, biting back laughter as I raise the snowball, aiming carefully.

"Ethan…" Jake's voice holds a warning tone. "What are you—"

Before he can finish, I hurl the snowball straight at him and it hits him square in the face with a muted thud. Snow explodes all over his cheeks and he gasps in shock.

"Surprise!" I shout, doubling over with laughter.

Jake stands frozen for a second, snow dripping off his face, his eyes wide in disbelief. He wipes the snow from his eyes and gives me a long, slow blink. "You… you did not just do that."

"Oh, but I did," I say, gasping for air between fits of laughter. "You should've seen your face!"

Jake shakes his head, but a grin is already spreading across his face. "You're dead. You realize that, right?"

"Worth it!" I call out, stepping back as I see him reach for something inside the studio.

"You better start running," Jake warns, now cackling as well. He grabs a handful of snow from the ledge outside his window. "Because payback's coming!"

As I roll on the ground, roaring with laughter so hard I can barely breathe, I hear a loud thud behind me. I look up, wiping tears from my eyes, only to see Jake, now fully awake, standing next to an absolutely massive snowball—seriously, it's the size of a cannonball.

Jake smirks down at me, his eyes gleaming with mischief.

I notice that he's not wearing a shirt under his unzipped coat. His six-pack from high school is still

F. A. SENG

intact and I'm pretty sure he's not wearing anything under those pajama pants.

"You thought you were safe, huh?" he says, hefting the snowball in both hands like it weighs nothing.

My laughter immediately dies down as I stare at the enormous snowball he's holding above his head. "Jake, wait… we can talk about this!"

But it's too late. Jake hurls the snowball straight at me and I barely manage to roll out of the way as it hits the ground with a heavy thump, sending snow flying everywhere. I jump to my feet, brushing snow off my jacket. "That thing could've knocked me out!" I shout, trying to suppress my grin.

Jake throws his head back and laughs. "You started this, remember?"

I grin, already scooping up another handful of snow. "Yeah, but I didn't realize I was dealing with a snowball expert!"

"Well, now you know," Jake says, packing another snowball. "What should we do next, oh fearless snow warrior?"

I look around the snow-covered ground, inspiration striking. "You know what?" I say, glancing over at Jake. "We should build a snowman. But not just any snowman—let's make it look like Brody."

Jake snorts, shaking his head. "Brody? Our Brody? The one who always steals the last slice of pizza?"

"Exactly," I say, already forming the base of the snowman. "We'll give him a giant head and tiny little legs. He'll look ridiculous."

Jake grins, clearly loving the idea. "It's going to be great," he says, but then glances down at his bare chest and pajama pants. "Maybe I should, uh, get dressed first?"

I smile and nod. "Yeah, you might want to. I'm not sure the snowball army will be intimidated by your six-pack."

Jake winks and jogs inside to change. "Don't start without me!" he calls through the open window.

"I won't!" I shout back, already starting to shape the base of our masterpiece.

A minute later, Jake returns, fully dressed in jeans and a black sweatshirt. He rubs his hands together, looking ready for action. "Alright, let's make Brody proud—or, you know, mock him endlessly."

We work together, rolling huge snowballs for the base and stacking them up. In no time, we've crafted a towering snowman with an oversized head and scrawny little legs. I give him a goofy, crooked smile made out of sticks and Jake grabs an old hat from the porch to plop on top.

Jake steps back, studying our creation. "That's disturbingly accurate."

I crack up, pointing at the snowman. "It's exactly how he looks when he's trying to lie about finishing the pizza."

Jake laughs, clearly enjoying this more than he expected. "Alright, so we've got Brody. Who's next?"

I grin, an idea forming in my mind. "We'll make another one... of Mrs. Jackson."

Jake freezes for a second before his face breaks into a mischievous grin. "Our high school history teacher? The one who gave me detention for yawning?"

"Yep, that's the one," I say, trying to keep a straight face. "We'll build Mrs. Jackson, then we'll bombard her with snowballs. Payback for all those years of lectures and essays on the French Revolution."

Jake chuckles, "I like how you think."

We quickly get to work on Mrs. Jackson, making her taller and more intimidating than Brody. I carefully craft a stern face out of stones and Jake wraps an old scarf around her neck, just like the ones she always wore. By the time we're done, she looks ready to lecture us about Napoleon.

"Perfect," I say, stepping back to appreciate our work. "It's like she's about to yell at us for not doing our homework."

Jake crosses his arms, looking proud. "And now... for revenge." He bends down, packing a snowball and tossing it lightly in his hand. "Ready?"

"Ready," I say, grinning as I make my own snowball.

On the count of three, we unleash a barrage of snowballs at Mrs. Jackson. Each hit sends snow flying off her face and body, soon her stone eyes are buried under a pile of snow.

"Take that, Mrs. J!" Jake shouts, breaking into laughter so hard he nearly misses his next shot.

"She gave me detention for talking too much in class," I say, pelting her with another snowball. "This is for all the essays on the French Revolution!"

"Oh, the essays!" Jake groans dramatically, launching a snowball right at her face. "She gave me a C+ on my Napoleon paper just because I didn't include enough sources!"

"Her expectations were too high!" I add, firing off another shot. "No one cared that much about Napoleon!"

Jake is practically doubled over with laughter now, snow flying everywhere as we unleash our playful fury on the snowman version of Mrs. Jackson. "If she could see us now, she'd give us detention for life."

I laugh so hard my sides hurt. "Totally worth it."

After a few more minutes of snowball warfare, Mrs. Jackson is completely buried in snow. We stand back, panting and cracking up over the mess we've created.

"Well, that was oddly satisfying," Jake says, wiping the snow off his gloves.

I nod, still catching my breath. "Definitely the best snowman-making session I've ever had."

Jake grins, his breath visible in the cold air. "Think we'll ever grow up?"

I shake my head, grinning back. "Nah, where's the fun in that?"

We spend the next hour building snowmen, giggling, and acting like we're kids again. By the time we're done, we've somehow managed to build a snowman even taller than either of us—at least seven feet tall.

"Think we overdid it?" I ask, glancing over at Jake, who's brushing snow off his gloves with a smug grin.

"Nah," he says, squinting at the towering snowman. "It's perfect. Besides, if we're going to have a snow battle, we need some defense."

I laugh, shaking my head. "Defense? Against who?"

Just then, three kids come sprinting up, their bright jackets standing out against the blanket of white snow. They stop in front of us, grinning from ear to ear. I recognize them right away—the neighborhood kids I helped earlier. They huddle together, whispering, like they're planning something big.

One of them, a little girl with blonde pigtails, steps forward and points at us dramatically. "We're soldiers and this is our territory!" she declares, her voice full of playful authority.

Jake crosses his arms, pretending to look serious. "Oh, is it now? I don't see your flag anywhere."

The other two boys nod, backing up the girl, as one of them yells, "We're gonna take it back!"

I raise an eyebrow at Jake, a smirk tugging at the corner of my mouth. "Well, looks like we've got a fight on our hands."

Jake bends down, scooping up a pile of snow and packing it into a solid snowball. "Let's see if they can handle this." Before I can say anything, he launches the snowball, hitting one of the boys squarely on the arm. The kid squeals in delight and immediately ducks behind a small snowbank.

"Oh, it's on now!" I say, grabbing a handful of snow and making my own snowball.

The kids let out playful war cries, diving behind their makeshift defenses as Jake and I exchange glances, grinning like idiots and then unleashing a flurry of snowballs in their direction. We throw at least a dozen in a matter of seconds.

The little girl tries to retaliate, tossing a snowball at us, but it barely makes it halfway before falling apart in the air. "You'll never take us down!" she shouts, laughing as she ducks behind the boys.

Jake is crying with laughter to the point that he almost falls over. "You call that an attack?" he teases, making another snowball and hurling it just over their heads, making sure not to actually hit them too hard.

One of the boys stands up, waving his arms. "Retreat! Retreat!" he yells, giggling as he scrambles away with the others.

"We'll be back!" another one calls over his shoulder as they run off, their laughter echoing in the frosty air. "We'll take our territory back, just you wait!"

I wipe snow from my face, grinning from ear to ear. "Well, looks like we won that round."

Jake nods, still chuckling. "Yeah, but they're probably plotting their revenge as we speak."

I glance up at our seven-foot snowman, towering over us like a silent sentinel. "Good thing we've got this guy to protect us," I joke, patting the snowman on the arm.

"Come on inside before we both freeze out here," Jake says, already making his way to the door of the studio.

I brush the snow off my coat, still smiling from our snowball fight. My hands are red and cold, but I don't care. The laughter, the ridiculous snowman, the battle with the kids—it's all been worth it. I follow Jake inside, the heat of the room hitting me immediately, like stepping into a hair dryer.

"Take a seat," Jake says, gesturing to the couch as he heads to the kitchen. "I'll make us some hot cocoa."

I nod and sink into the couch cushions, the coziness quickly seeping into my frozen body. While Jake is in the kitchen, I glance around his apartment, noticing the framed photos on the walls. There's one of him at an art exhibition, proudly standing next to one of his pieces. Another of him as a kid, smiling wide, missing a couple of front teeth. I smile, feeling like I'm seeing a part of Jake's world I hadn't before.

A few minutes later, Jake returns with two mugs, steam rising from the cocoa. He hands me one and the warmth immediately stings my frozen fingers as they begin to defrost.

"Here you go," he says, sitting beside me on the couch. "This should thaw us out."

I take a sip, the rich, sweet taste of chocolate filling my senses. "Mmm, this is good. You really know how to make a solid cup of cocoa."

Jake smiles, taking a sip from his own cup. "Thanks. I used to make it all the time when I was a kid after snowball fights like the one we just had."

I chuckle. "I forgot how fun that used to be. We really took those kids down, though."

Jake laughs, his eyes lighting up with that playful glint I've grown used to. "They didn't stand a chance, I mean, we're snowball professionals. They were amateurs."

I shake my head, smiling. "You're right. We might've traumatized them for life. They'll probably never challenge us again."

We keep talking and pealing with laughter about the snowman and the battle outside. The chocolatey aroma of cocoa fills the room and I can feel the heat spreading from my hands to the rest of my body. As we talk, I notice how close Jake has gotten. I don't know when it happened, but suddenly, our faces are only inches apart.

The conversation fades into the background as I become acutely aware of everything—his eyes, the faint scent of his cologne, the sound of his breathing. My heart starts pounding in my chest. I can feel his breath, light and delicate, brushing against my lips. My eyes drift over his face, noticing the small details I hadn't seen before. The tiny cut just under his left eye. The almost faded mole on his forehead. His lips are slightly parted and I can see the same realization dawning in his eyes.

I freeze, unsure of what to do next. The air between us feels heavy, charged with something neither of us can name. My heart races and I could swear his is, too. I feel the tension, the pull between us, I don't know if I should move closer or—

Suddenly, there's a loud knock at the door, shattering the moment.

Jake blinks, quickly pulling back and I sit up straighter, my pulse still racing. I clear my throat, trying to act like nothing just happened, but there's a small smile tugging at my lips and I see the same on Jake's face.

"Uh, I'll get that," Jake mutters, standing up a little too quickly.

I watch him head for the door, my heart still pounding in my chest. *Who the hell could that be right now?*

Jake opens the door and Tess is standing there, bundled up in a thick scarf, his cheeks red from the cold.

"Hey!" he greets, his voice chipper. "I thought I'd drop by since Ethan said he'd be here."

I swallow hard, trying to force myself to act normal. "Hey, Tess," I say, giving him a wave. "Didn't expect you to show up so soon."

He walks in, oblivious to the tension that had just been between me and Jake, plops down on the couch, sighing contentedly. "It's freezing out there! I could really use some of that cocoa."

eleven

I'm sitting on my couch, mindlessly scrolling through my phone, when the thought of texting Jake crosses my mind. It's been a while since we hung out, after the snowball fight and the almost... moment in his studio, I can't stop thinking about him. Smiling at the memory, I quickly type out a message:

Me:

> Hey are you free tonight?

I wait, hoping he isn't too busy with his art. Jake works non-stop when he has an exhibition coming up, but maybe, just maybe, he'll have some time. A few seconds later, my phone buzzes. It's Jake.

Jake:

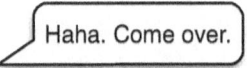

I'm just working on my next exhibition.

My face falls a little and I send back a sad emoji, figuring that's the end of it for today. Almost immediately, my phone buzzes again.

Jake:

Haha. Come over.

Grinning, a rush of excitement surges through me. I don't hesitate to reply.

Me:

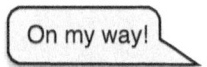

On my way!

I grab my jacket and head out the door. There's no way I'm missing out on seeing Jake today, especially with how things have been between us lately. Something feels different and I can't shake the feeling that we might just be heading somewhere… deeper.

I make my way to Jake's studio, my hands stuffed in my pockets and the cold biting at my face. When I reach the door, I pause for a second, feeling that familiar buzz of anticipation I always get when I'm about to see him. I knock lightly, then push the door open.

Jake is sitting on a couch, leaning forward in conversation with a woman I don't recognize. She's elegant, with sharp features and an air of confidence that radiates off her. They both turn to look at me as I step inside.

"Ethan! You made it," Jake says, his voice a little too bright, almost forced. There's something off and I can't place it. He gets up from the couch and walks over, giving me a quick smile before gesturing to the woman. "Ethan, this is Maria T. Foster. She's organizing my exhibition. Maria, this is Ethan."

Maria smiles politely, extending her hand. "Nice to meet you, Ethan. I've heard quite a bit about you."

I raise an eyebrow as I shake her hand. "Good things, I hope?"

She chuckles in a hushed tone, however, there's something behind her eyes that I can't quite read. "Of course."

There's a brief, almost awkward silence as I glance between the two of them. I'm not sure what to say next, so thank god Jake quickly jumps in. "Uh, do you guys want some coffee? I can make a pot."

"Yeah, sure," I say and Maria nods in agreement.

"Alright, I'll be right back," Jake says, heading into the small kitchen off to the side of the studio.

As soon as he leaves, the room feels… different. Maria's gaze shifts back to me and I can feel the weight of her eyes on me, studying me. I try to act casual, sitting down on the opposite end of the couch from her.

"So," I start, just trying to break the tension, "how's the exhibition planning going?"

Maria gives a small, disingenuous smile. "It's going well. Jake's very talented, as you probably already know."

I nod, feeling the need to agree, but also sensing an edge to her tone. "Yeah, he really is. I've seen a lot of his work. It's… incredible."

Her smile grows a bit tighter. "You seem to know him well."

There's something in the way she says that—like there's more to the statement than just casual curiosity. I clear my throat. "Yeah, we've been friends for a while now."

"I see," Maria says with her voice still soft, however, her eyes are still sharp. There's a brief pause before she adds, "It's nice that he has someone to rely on. I imagine this exhibition has been a lot of pressure for him."

I can't tell if she's genuinely concerned for Jake or if there's something more under the surface. But I play along. "Yeah, it's been a lot, but I think he'll pull it off. He always does."

Maria nods slowly, her gaze shifting toward the kitchen where Jake is. She's quiet for a moment, then glances back at me. "You two seem... close."

I blink, a little caught off guard by her directness. "Uh, yeah, I guess so. We've been hanging out a lot lately."

She smiles again and this time there's a flicker of something else. Is that... jealousy? Her eyes linger on me for just a beat too long and I shift uncomfortably in my seat.

Just as I'm about to respond, Jake reappears from the kitchen, balancing three mugs of coffee in his hands. "Coffee's ready!" he announces, seemingly unaware of the strange tension that has settled in the room.

He hands me my cup first, his fingers brushing mine for a split second sending a small jolt through me. I quickly take the mug, hoping neither of them notices my reaction. Jake then hands a cup to Maria, who accepts it with a gracious nod, though her eyes are still on me.

"Thanks," she says, her tone a little cooler than before.

Jake plops down next to me, his knee barely grazing mine and I can feel the warmth radiating from his body. "So, what were you guys talking about?" he asks.

Maria takes a slow sip of her coffee, her eyes flicking between us. "Just getting to know Ethan a little better," she replies smoothly.

Jake smiles, oblivious of the subtle undercurrent. "Well, I can tell you that you'll be hearing plenty more about him if you hang around me long enough."

I feel my face heat up at that and Maria's expression doesn't change. If anything, her smile seems more forced now. "I'm sure," she says, her tone a bit stiffer.

An awkward silence follows and I find myself fidgeting with my coffee cup, unsure how to navigate this strange dynamic. Jake, still completely clueless, keeps the conversation going.

"So, Maria, do you think we're on track for the exhibition?" Jake asks, taking a sip of his coffee.

Maria's eyes linger on him for a moment before she nods. "Yes, everything seems to be in place. We just need to finalize a few details, other than that we should be good to go."

Jake sighs with relief. "That's great. I've been stressing over it for weeks."

"I can imagine," Maria says, her tone softening slightly. "You'll do fine, Jake. Your work speaks for itself."

Jake smiles at that, however, I notice how Maria's gaze drifts back toward me. It's subtle, but there's something there—something I can't quite pin down. Whether it's curiosity, jealousy, or both, it makes me feel a little… uncomfortable.

The silence stretches for a moment after Jake gets back to work, leaving Maria and me sitting across from each other, both of us awkwardly sipping our coffee. The warmth of the cup in my hands feels like the only thing grounding me. I don't know what to say. She keeps glancing at me, like she's waiting for me to make the first move, so I figure I'll break the ice.

"So, uh…" I clear my throat, trying not to let my voice falter. "What do you do, Maria? Besides exhibitions, I mean."

Her eyes meet mine, a flicker of curiosity behind her composed expression. She tilts her head slightly, the corner of her mouth curling into a small smile. "Well, exhibitions are pretty much it. I've been doing this for the past eight years."

"Eight years? That's a long time," I say, raising my eyebrows. "You must love what you do."

Maria gives a small shrug, her tone almost dismissive. "It's alright. It keeps me busy and I've had the privilege of working with some talented artists."

There's a strange edge in her words. She glances over at Jake, who's busy tweaking a painting across the room, completely absorbed in his work. She turns back to me, her eyes assessing. "What about you, Ethan? What do you do?"

I shift in my seat, feeling like I'm being examined. "Oh, nothing as exciting as organizing exhibitions, that's for sure. I work as a marketing executive for a logistics company."

Her smile doesn't waver. "A marketing executive, huh? Sounds… practical."

I chuckle, knowing it's not the most glamorous job. "Yeah, it's a lot of numbers and strategy. Not exactly art, but it keeps me on my toes. Pays the bills, you know?"

She nods, however, it's clear she's not impressed. There's a brief pause and I feel the need to turn the conversation back toward her, just to keep things moving. "So, you've been organizing Jake's exhibitions for a while now?"

Maria leans back slightly, her posture is relaxed and there is judgment in her eyes. "Yes. I've managed all of Jake's exhibitions since he started. He's one of my more… consistent clients."

"Wow, that's impressive," I say, trying to keep the conversation light. "I didn't realize you'd been working together for that long."

She smiles, but there's something in the way she says her next words that feels pointed. "Yes, Jake and I have a good understanding. We've built quite a history together."

I catch the implication—whether it's intentional or not and I'm not sure how to respond. There's an odd strain hanging in the air, like Maria is staking a claim without actually saying it. I glance over at Jake, who's still completely focused on his work.

"That's great," I say, keeping my voice neutral. "It must be nice to have that kind of long-term partnership."

Maria's eyes linger on me for a moment longer than necessary before she finally takes another sip of her coffee. "It is. Jake's work is... unique. He has a vision that not many artists have."

I nod, feeling the need to agree. "Yeah, he's incredibly talented."

There's another moment of pause and I can feel the weight of her gaze again, like she's sizing me up. It's like she's trying to figure out where I fit into Jake's life—and whether she likes it or not.

"So," Maria says, her tone shifting slightly, "how long have you and Jake known each other?"

"A while now," I reply, feeling the need to be vague. "We met in high school and we weren't super close then, it's only been recently that we've been hitting it off."

Maria raises an eyebrow, clearly curious. "Hitting it off, huh?"

"Yeah," I say, trying not to sound defensive. "We've seen each other almost everyday since I got in from New York."

Her smile falls flat this time and I can feel the unease rising again. It's subtle, but the conversation feels like a chess game and I'm not entirely sure what her next move is going to be. Before I can say anything else, Jake calls out from across the room.

"Hey, you two! Want to come see what I've been working on?" Jake shouts from the other room.

I'm grateful for the distraction. I stand up, glancing at Maria as she slowly rises from the couch. Her expression remains polite, but there's still that underlying tension in her eyes.

"Sure," I say, making my way over to Jake's work area. "Let's see what you've got."

As Jake adjusts a canvas, I take a moment to admire the vibrant colors splashed across it. The pieces around the studio all feel alive, bursting with emotion and energy. I turn to him, feeling a surge of excitement. "So, how can I help you with all this? What do you need?"

Jake pauses, wiping his hands on a rag. "Well, even though my exhibitions are well received, I want my work to spread even further. I want people to really see it, you know?"

I nod, totally understanding where he's coming from. "Absolutely. Getting your art out there is crucial."

Maria chimes in, crossing her arms. "We've been holding exhibitions for quite some time now. We've had a few good buyers, we're just thinking about going larger. Expanding the audience."

"Going larger sounds like a great idea," I say, feeling the gears in my head start to turn. "I've been in the marketing industry for a long time and I think I can help you with this."

Jake looks intrigued. "Really? What do you have in mind?"

I lean in a little, excitement bubbling over. "Well, first, we can create a robust marketing plan that targets both local and wider audiences. We need to promote your exhibitions across different platforms—social media, local art blogs, and even community boards. The more visibility, the better."

Jake nods, his brow furrowed as he absorbs my words. "That makes sense. I've always focused more on the art than the marketing side of things."

"Exactly," I continue. "We can also organize some artist talks or Q&A sessions during the exhibitions. It gives people a chance to connect with you and your work on a personal level. It'll draw more attention."

Maria seems to lean into the idea. "That could definitely engage the audience more. People love hearing the story behind the art."

"Right!" I say, feeling the momentum build. "What if we set up a few guided tours? We could bring in local schools, art clubs, and community groups. It'll give them a chance to experience your work up close and they might even become future buyers."

Jake's eyes light up, I can see the excitement building in him. "I love that idea! It's a way to create a community around the art."

I smile, thrilled to see his enthusiasm. "And we can't forget about advertisements. We could do some targeted online ads and even print some flyers for local coffee shops and galleries. Get the word out everywhere."

Maria chimes in, her voice animated now. "We could even partner with local businesses for cross-promotions. It might help create a buzz."

"Exactly!" I say, feeling like I'm on a roll. "After we get everything set up, we can do a big launch event for the next exhibition. Something that will really grab attention."

Jake nods vigorously, clearly caught up in the vision. "That sounds amazing! We could have live music, maybe even invite some local food vendors."

"Now you're talking!" I laugh. "It would be an event people won't want to miss."

Maria crosses her arms, a satisfied smile spreading across her face. "This is sounding more and more promising. If we execute this right, we could really expand Jake's reach."

I feel a wave of anticipation wash over me as I glance between them. "I think we can do this. With a little teamwork, we can make this the best exhibition yet."

Jake grins, his eyes sparkling with newfound hope. "Thanks, Ethan. I really appreciate you stepping in like this. I've been so focused on the art that I never thought about how to reach a broader audience."

"No problem at all," I say, feeling a rush of purpose. "I'm just glad I can help. Let's make this happen."

I glance over at Jake and Maria, feeling a mix of eagerness and curiosity. "Hey, do you think I could see the paintings you're planning to put up in the exhibition?" I ask, genuinely intrigued by what Jake has been working on.

Maria hesitates, her posture stiffening a little. "I'm not sure if that's a good idea," she says cautiously. "You haven't officially joined the exhibition team yet."

I'm about to nod, figuring I can wait, when Jake cuts her off. "Oh, come on, Maria. There's no issue with

Ethan seeing them." His voice is casual, brushing aside her concerns.

Maria opens her mouth to object, but Jake shoots her a reassuring look. "Trust me, it's fine. Ethan can give us some fresh insight. He knows what he's talking about."

She sighs, clearly frustrated, though remains quiet. After a moment, she gives a reluctant nod. "Fine. Let's go."

I follow Jake and Maria to the back room of the studio, where the paintings are stored. As Jake unlocks the door, I can sense Maria's quiet irritation, though she says nothing as we step inside.

The room is lined with canvases, some large, others more modest in size. I count seventeen pieces, each one vibrant and distinct in its own way. Jake grins, guiding me through them like a personal tour guide. "There's a lot here. Each of these pieces has its own story."

We move from one painting to the next, with Jake enthusiastically explaining his inspiration for each one. Maria trails a few steps behind, her gaze shifting between Jake and I.

Then I pause, my eyes drawn to one particular painting—a forest scene, with light filtering through the dense trees in a way that feels almost magical. There's something familiar about it, a distant memory tugging at the edges of my mind.

F. A. SENG

Before I can say anything, Jake grins. "Yup, that's the one."

I raise an eyebrow, with a half-smile on. "No way… this is the forest, isn't it?"

Jake chuckles and nods. "The one and only. The forest behind our school where everyone used to sneak off with their partners after dark. You remember, right?"

I can't help but grin. "Yeah, I remember. It was the ultimate spot for those 'adventures.' How could anyone forget?"

Jake and I exchange a look, the shared memory pulling us back to those carefree, mischievous teenage years. We laugh, the kind of laughter that comes from reliving something so ridiculous, yet cherished.

Maria, however, doesn't share in the amusement. Her posture is stiff, arms crossed tightly over her chest. She clears her throat, visibly annoyed. "What's so funny?" she asks, though it's clear she doesn't really care for an answer.

Jake glances over at her. "Oh, it's just this forest. It's kind of a… landmark from our high school days."

I smile, adding, "Yeah, everyone who went to our school knew about it. It was the go-to place for sneaking off with your boyfriend or girlfriend. Kind of legendary, really."

Maria forces a small smile, like really forced. She doesn't seem to find the story quite as entertaining as

137

Jake and I do. In fact, if anything, she looks... irritated. I can see the tension in her posture, the way her jaw tightens.

Jake, being the golden retriever that he is, still doesn't seem to notice. He's still caught up in the memory. "There was one time when I almost got caught by Mr. Carlson. He was walking his dog near the edge of the woods and we barely managed to duck behind those bushes in time." He pointed to a group of bushes in the painting.

I burst out laughing. "Oh my God, I heard about that!"

We both laugh again, the shared nostalgia warming the moment, yet Maria's mood seems to sour even more. I can almost feel her resentment building in the silence. It's as if our inside jokes have drawn a line between us, one she can't cross.

She stays quiet for a beat longer then speaks, her tone carefully neutral. "It must be nice," she says, though her words carry a certain weight. "To have those kinds of memories."

I glance at her, sensing there's more behind her words than she's letting on. I give her a polite smile, not wanting to make things more uncomfortable, though the air feels thicker between us.

Jake shrugs. "Yeah, it was. Good times."

Maria doesn't respond and we continue through the rest of the paintings. The easy laughter between Jake and me fades into a quieter, more awkward atmosphere. Every time I glance at Maria, I can't help but notice the irritation in her eyes, as if she wishes she could be the one sharing those moments with Jake.

twelve

I'm tearing through the stuff in my room, tossing clothes and papers aside, trying to find my damn keys. Where the hell did I leave them? The exhibition starts in less than an hour and I'm nowhere near ready. I rummage through my desk drawer, shoving old receipts and random junk out of the way.

"Ethan!" Jamie's voice startles me and I turn to see her standing in the doorway, arms crossed, giving me one of her classic 'what are you doing?' looks. "Where are you headed in such a hurry?"

"The exhibition," I say, still half-distracted, flipping through piles of papers. "It's starting soon and I need to get there before anything kicks off."

Jamie raises an eyebrow, leaning against the doorframe. "Why are you always this last-minute?"

I grin as I finally find my keys under a stack of notebooks. "You know me. I thrive on the adrenaline."

Jamie laughs, but then her expression shifts to curiosity. "So, how many people are you guys expecting at this thing?"

I glance up at her, tossing my keys into my pocket. "Today? Probably around 30 or 40. It's the first day, so it'll be a bit quieter."

"Thirty or forty?" she repeats, nodding thoughtfully. "That sounds decent."

I straighten up, pulling on my jacket. "Yeah, but that's just today. Tomorrow's a whole different story. We're looking at anywhere between 200 and 600 people coming through."

Jamie's eyes widen, her jaw practically hitting the floor. "Wait, what? Six hundred people? For Jake's exhibition?"

I can't help smirking at her reaction, standing a little taller, puffing my chest out with pride. "Yup. We've been working for the last two days, almost 20 hours each day, to ensure that this exhibit is the best it can be. Fine-tuned the whole setup, ran some targeted ads and pulled in a few of my contacts. It's not just a small gallery show anymore—it's an event."

Jamie blinks at me, still processing what I've just said. "Ethan, that's insane. Jake's never had more than 60 people at one of his exhibitions. This is… huge."

I grin, feeling the excitement build up inside me. "Yeah, well, I knew we could push it further. Jake's work is incredible, I think it just needed the right kind of audience. So, I made sure to get the word out. Plus, some of the people coming are major players—gallery owners, art collectors. If this goes well, it could open a lot of doors for him."

Jamie shakes her head in disbelief, staring at me like she doesn't even recognize the guy standing in front of her. "You really pulled all this together?"

"Of course I did," I say, throwing on my scarf and grabbing my bag. "It's all about making connections, finding the right people. Once you do that, it's easy to get the momentum going. Plus, I've been talking to some artists from other cities. They're coming too."

Jamie stands there, her mouth hanging open for a second before smiling. "You're seriously something, you know that? Jake owes you big time."

I laugh, waving her off. "Nah, it's a team effort. Jake's work speaks for itself. I'm just helping get it in front of the right people."

Jamie steps back, still looking a little dazed. "Well, you're gonna kill it. I know you will."

"I hope so," I say, giving her a quick grin before heading toward the door. "But I gotta run now, or I'll be late. Wish me luck!"

Jamie looks directly at me, still smiling. "You don't need luck. Just go knock 'em dead."

I flash her a quick thumbs-up, already halfway out the door. "Thanks! I'll fill you in later!"

Before she can say anything else, I sprint down the stairs, waving her a quick goodbye as I run out the front door, excitement buzzing in my veins. Today is going to be huge. I can feel it.

I'm sprinting down the street, my heart pounding in my chest as I make my way to the studio. The cold air stings my cheeks, but I don't care—I'm too hyped to feel it. As I turn the corner, I spot Jake and Maria standing near the entrance, both of them looking like they've been waiting for me.

Jake is pacing, his hands shoved in his pockets, but the moment he sees me, he grins. "There he is! You ready?"

I slow down, trying to catch my breath and flash him a cocky grin. "Ready? Jake, I was born ready."

He laughs, shaking his head. "Good, 'cause this is it. Big day."

Maria stands there with her arms crossed, rolling her eyes at both of us. "Stop wasting time, boys. Let's get this thing started. We've got guests coming in less than 20 minutes and I don't want to be caught off guard."

I smirk at her. Maria is always the practical one, keeping us on track. "Alright, alright," I say, brushing off the front of my jacket. "I'm good. Let's do this."

The entrance is mostly empty, just a few managing staff setting things up making sure the guest list is ready and some early onlookers lingering by the door. I can feel the calm before the storm, the air thick with anticipation. The setup looks fantastic, with banners promoting Jake's work, sleek lighting lining the gallery's entrance and art pieces just visible through the glass walls. This is going to be big.

Jake glances over at me, his expression a little more serious now. "You sure everything's in place? You've been handling the invites and contacts. I've been too focused on the art—I barely know who's even coming."

I give him a confident nod. "Trust me. It's all good. Got the big names confirmed, a few gallery owners, some collectors. It's going to be a full house starting tomorrow. Today, we keep it cool. You just focus on greeting people, Maria and I will handle the logistics."

Maria raises an eyebrow. "By 'cool,' you mean smoothly organized and running on time, right?"

I shoot her a playful look. "Yeah, yeah, smoothly. I've got it covered."

She nods, satisfied, then claps her hands together. "Alright, let's move, people! No more standing around. Jake, get in position at the door. Ethan, keep an eye on the guest list. I don't want anyone important slipping by."

I take my spot near the entrance as Jake moves to greet guests, Maria already flitting around like a professional, directing people and making sure everything is in order. We have about 20 minutes to spare, so I keep myself busy, double-checking the guest list and keeping an eye on the staff who are setting up the final touches.

As I scroll through the names on my phone, Jake glances over at me. "I'm nervous, man."

I laugh, shaking my head. "You? Nervous? Come on, you've done this before."

"Not like this," he says, glancing toward the empty entranceway. "Not with this many people, not with collectors and gallery owners showing up."

"Hey, relax," I say, giving him a reassuring pat on the back. "You've got this. Your work is amazing. Once they see it, they're gonna be blown away. You just gotta smile and shake a few hands. Let me worry about everything else."

He smiles, but I can still see a little tension in his shoulders. "Thanks. I just hope I don't screw it up."

"You won't," I say firmly. "Just be yourself. That's what people are here for. They're not just buying the art; they're buying you."

Maria appears beside us, glancing at her watch. "Alright, guys, game faces on. Guests will be here any minute."

Sure enough, within a few minutes, the first few guests start trickling in. Jake straightens his posture, smoothing down his shirt as he steps up to greet them.

"Welcome!" Jake says, his voice warm and inviting as he shakes hands with the first couple of people. "Thank you so much for coming. We're excited to have you here."

Maria, ever the professional, guides the guests toward the exhibition space with a polite smile. "This way, please. The exhibition is just through here. Feel free to browse and Jake will be happy to answer any questions about his work."

Meanwhile, I stay near the door, making sure I keep tabs on who's coming in. My phone buzzes occasionally with updates from people running late or confirming they're on their way. I make a mental note of every gallery owner and collector who enters, ready to connect them with Jake when the time is right.

As more people file in, the energy in the room picks up. I spot a couple of familiar faces—people I've invited personally, some with serious clout in the art world. I make sure to greet them, steering them in Jake's direction when I can.

"Ethan," Maria whispers as she passes by me, her voice low but urgent, "have you seen the big fish, yet? Any of the major collectors?"

"Not yet," I reply, scanning the room again. "But they'll be here. This is just the warm-up."

Jake catches my eye from across the room and gives me a thumbs-up, his confidence seeming to grow with each handshake and introduction. I nod back, feeling the pride swell in my chest. This is going better than I'd hoped and I can't wait for the real crowd to hit tomorrow.

Maria comes up beside me again, watching as Jake charms another group of guests. "You did good, Ethan," she says quietly, her eyes still on Jake. "This is gonna be huge."

I smile, unable to hide my excitement. "It already is."

* * *

I'm keeping a close eye on everything as the exhibition picks up and more guests arrive, making sure people are where they need to be and that everything runs smoothly. Jake's in his element, shaking hands, talking about his work, and generally being the star of the show. His easygoing charm is cranked up to full volume and I can see how comfortable he is in this space.

That's when I spot them—a group of three men and two women walking toward Jake. They're dressed in that artsy, effortlessly cool way that screams "artist." I watch as they hug Jake, greeting him with kisses on both cheeks, laughing and chatting like they've known each other forever. They're all smiles, like this is a reunion they've been waiting for.

Jake notices me watching from across the room and waves me over. "Ethan! Come here," he calls, his grin widening as he beckons me to join them.

I hesitate for a second, not wanting to interrupt, but Jake's eyes stay on me, so I make my way over.

"Ethan," Jake says, slinging his arm around my shoulder as I reach the group, "I want you to meet some very important people."

The group turns their attention to me, all of them with warm smiles.

"This is Ethan," Jake introduces me, his voice full of pride. "He's been the mastermind behind tonight's exhibition. Seriously couldn't have done any of this without him."

I feel a small flush creep up my neck. "Oh, it's nothing," I say, rubbing the back of my neck. "Just making sure things run seamlessly."

Jake continues, "Ethan, these are people from the very first art class I ever took and we all have grown really close since!"

One of the women, a tall, striking brunette with a bright smile, steps forward and shakes my hand. "It's nice to meet you, Ethan. I'm Sophia," she says cordially. "Jake's told us a lot about you."

"Yeah," one of the men chimes in, a guy with wild, curly hair and a thick scarf draped around his neck. "Jake says you're the one making sure this whole thing doesn't fall apart." He laughs, giving me a playful nudge. "We owe you a drink for keeping this guy in line."

I laugh nervously, glancing at Jake. "He's not that hard to handle."

Jake grins. "See? Ethan gets me."

The rest of the group chimes in with greetings. There's Luca, the curly-haired guy, Ava, the other woman with short, platinum blonde hair and round glasses that make her look like a professor. The last two are Carlos and Emile, both artists who radiate a calm, almost serene energy.

"These guys are some of the most talented artists I've ever seen," Jake says, smiling at the group.

"We try," Carlos says with a chuckle. "But honestly, Jake, you've come a long way. Your work tonight is phenomenal."

Everyone nods in agreement and the conversation quickly turns to the art in the exhibition. They start discussing the pieces, throwing around terms like "composition," "visual tension," and "form," all of them nodding along like they're in their own world.

I stand there, smiling and nodding politely, although after a few minutes, I start feeling out of place. They're talking about techniques, inspirations, and collaborations I don't fully understand. Even though I appreciate Jake's art, I'm not fluent in the language they're speaking.

Jake catches my eye at one point, I try to give him a reassuring smile, but I know this isn't my scene. I'm not part of this inner circle of artists and I don't have much to contribute to the conversation. The group is deep into a discussion about the way light interacts with the textures in one of Jake's pieces and I realize I'm just standing there like a third wheel.

I clear my throat and glance at my phone, pretending to check for messages. "Hey guys," I say, stepping back a bit, "I should probably get back to, uh, checking on the guests. Just want to make sure everything's still running smoothly."

Jake looks at me, his expression softening a bit. "You sure? You don't have to go."

I smile, shaking my head. "Yeah, no worries. You're in good hands with these guys."

Sophia gives me a kind smile. "It was great meeting you, Ethan. Thanks for all the work you've done."

"Same here," I reply, backing away. "Enjoy the exhibition. I'll catch up with you all later."

Jake gives me a quick nod of understanding before turning back to the group, I can already hear them picking up the conversation where they left off. As I walk away, I feel a slight sense of relief. Art talk isn't really my thing and besides, I have work to do.

I stand off to the side, scanning the room, pretending to be focused on something important. In reality, I'm just giving myself a little space to breathe. The art talk had gotten intense back there. Jake's surrounded by his people—people who speak his language, know the ins and outs of composition and light. And I… well, I'm just the guy who makes sure everything stays on track.

I see Jake laughing with them, but then out of the corner of my eye, I notice him glance over at me. For a second, I think he'll go back to the conversation, instead, he excuses himself from the group and walks straight toward me, that easy smile of his loosening as he approaches.

"Hey," he says quietly, stopping in front of me. "You good?"

I look up, a little surprised. "Yeah, yeah, I'm fine," I say quickly, trying to brush it off. "Just, you know, checking in on things. Making sure everything's running well."

Jake frowns, studying me for a second. He's not buying it. "Ethan, you sure?"

I force a smile. "I promise. It's all good."

Jake tilts his head, his eyes narrowing playfully. "Uh-huh. You forget who you're talking to? I can tell when you're feeling out of place."

I let out a small chuckle, shaking my head. "Okay, fine. Maybe I was a little... lost back there. You guys were speaking a whole different language. I didn't want to just stand there like a doofus."

Jake grins, his eyes lighting up. "Well, that's because you weren't supposed to stay there. Come with me."

I blink, confused. "Where are we going?"

"Tour time," he says, stepping to the side and motioning for me to follow him. "I've been waiting for the right moment to show you around. This is the V-VIP treatment I've reserved just for you."

I can't help but giggle, following him as we weave through the crowd. "V-VIP, huh? I'm honored."

"You should be," Jake says, flashing me a grin over his shoulder. "Not everyone gets the behind-the-scenes artist's tour."

We start walking through the gallery, moving from one painting to the next. Jake stops at each piece, explaining the inspiration behind it, what he was trying to capture, how he used certain techniques to get the effect he wanted. It's amazing, honestly, hearing him talk about his work with so much passion and depth. I've seen most of these pieces before, but now they feel different, like they have more weight, more meaning.

"This one," Jake says, stopping in front of a massive abstract painting with bold reds and oranges, "is all about chaos. I was going through some stuff when I painted it—felt like everything in my life was spinning out of control."

I look at it, seeing the erratic brushstrokes, the tension in the lines. "Yeah, I can feel that," I say quietly. "It's intense."

Jake nods, his expression softening. "Yeah. It helped me work through a lot though. Art has a way of doing that, you know?"

As we move to the next painting, I realize that without even thinking about it, Jake and I have started holding hands. It feels natural, like we've done it a thousand times before. I don't pull away and neither does he. Instead, we keep walking, his fingers laced through mine as we wander through the exhibition.

"So," I say, breaking the comfortable silence, "what's next for you? After this exhibition, I mean."

Jake glances at me, a small smile playing on his lips. "Honestly? I don't know. I've been thinking a lot about what's next. I've got a few ideas, but nothing set in stone yet. This whole thing... it's been huge for me. I want to make sure it's just the beginning, you know?"

I nod. "Yeah, I get that. I think tonight's going to open a lot of doors for you, though. I mean, you've got some big names in here. People are paying attention."

Jake's hand tightens slightly around mine as we stop in front of another painting. "That's thanks to you, you know. You've done more for me than I could ever ask for."

I shake my head, smiling. "I just made sure everything went smoothly. You're the one with the talent, Jake. I'm just here to make sure the world sees it."

He looks at me for a moment, his eyes lightening. "Still, I couldn't have done it without you."

For a second, I don't know what to say. There's something about the way he's looking at me, something unspoken, but saturated with meaning. I can feel the weight of his words and it makes my heart beat just a little faster.

We walk to the next painting, still holding hands and I try to steer the conversation into safer territory. "So, what do you think the crowd's going to look like tomorrow? We've got a pretty decent turnout today, but I bet it's going to be packed."

Jake grins. "I hope so. I mean, we've got the space and with the buzz we've been building, it should be wild."

"Wild is one way to put it," I smile. "It'll be good. I've got a feeling tomorrow's going to be insane—in a good way."

Jake glances at me again, that same adorable smile on his lips. "As long as you're there, I know it'll be good."

thirteen

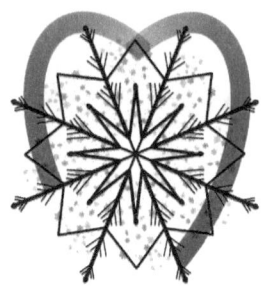

Day two of the exhibition is set to kick off at exactly 9 a.m. and we've gathered early at the studio to make sure everything is perfect. The energy in the room is intense—excitement, nerves, and a bit of tension hang in the air. We've spent hours upon hours preparing for this moment and now it's finally happening.

I'm standing near the entrance, checking the guest list on my phone one last time as Maria goes over some last-minute details with the staff. Jake is pacing a little, clearly hyped, but trying to keep it cool. His hair is still slightly messy, like he's run his hands through it a thousand times in the last hour. It makes him look even more like the effortlessly cool artist everyone expects him to be.

Maria walks over to us, her phone in hand, a huge grin plastered on her face. "Guys," she says, her eyes twinkling. "I've got some amazing news. The response from the invitees has been incredible. We're looking at possibly reaching 300 people by the end of the exhibition."

I watch Jake's reaction as she speaks and the moment the number hits his ears, his whole face lights up. "Three hundred?" he says, almost in disbelief. "Are you serious?"

Maria nods, her grin growing wider. "Yup. That's just from the early interest. If the chatter keeps building like it has been, we could easily hit that number—or even more."

Jake runs a hand through his hair, his eyes wide with excitement. "Holy shit," he mutters, a massive smile breaking across his face. "I mean, I knew it would be good, but this is… wow."

I can't help smiling too, watching him. The pure joy on his face, the way he's practically vibrating with energy—it's contagious. My stomach does a little flip and suddenly I feel this weird mix of pride and nerves. Seeing this side of Jake—so excited, so thrilled—it gives me butterflies.

"Jake, you're about to blow people away," I say, trying to keep my voice steady. "This is all you. They're coming because they know how good you are."

He looks at me, his smile still wide, but his eyes softening. "No, Ethan, this is because of you, too. I couldn't have gotten this far without you. Seriously."

I shake my head, feeling the heat rise in my face. "Nah, I just made sure people showed up. You're the one with the talent."

Jake steps closer, still grinning. "You made sure the right people showed up. And that's what makes all the difference."

Maria, watching us with a knowing smile, clears her throat. "Okay. We've still got work to do. Guests are gonna start rolling in soon and I need both of you focused."

Jake chuckles, giving her a playful salute. "Yes, ma'am."

I laugh too, but my stomach is still flipping as Jake turns back to the entrance, his whole body practically humming with anticipation. He looks like he's ready to take on the world, honestly, he kind of is.

Maria taps her phone again, checking the time. "Alright, it's almost showtime. Ethan, make sure the guest list is up and running. I'll handle the staff and Jake... just keep being the charming artist genius everyone's here to see."

Jake shoots her a grin. "Charming genius? I can do that."

I roll my eyes, unable to stop myself from laughing. "Modest, too."

He nudges me with his shoulder, that playful gleam in his eye. "What can I say? I've got it all."

Maria sighs dramatically. "Alright, boys. Focus. This is it."

As the clock ticks closer to 9 a.m., I can feel the buzz in the room intensify. The butterflies in my stomach don't stop—they just flutter faster, especially whenever I glance at Jake. He's on fire, grinning like a kid on Christmas morning, his enthusiasm radiating off him.

The exhibition has barely started and already the place is flowing with energy. People are pouring in through the doors and within the first hour, we've got 267 guests. I keep glancing at the counters the staff are using to keep track and it's wild how fast the numbers are climbing. We'd hoped for a big crowd, but this? This is way beyond expectations.

I'm standing near the entrance, watching as the staff greet people, handing out brochures and guiding them through the gallery. The space that felt large and open an hour ago now seems packed, with people crowding around Jake's artwork, pointing, elated by the talent. It's a success, no doubt about it, but it's also becoming a bit chaotic.

I catch sight of Maria weaving through the crowd, her expression a mix of awe and mild panic. She reaches me, breathless, holding her phone like it's a lifeline.

"Ethan," she says, half-laughing, half-shaking her head, "your idea worked. And when I say it worked, I mean it's way too efficient."

I grin, a bit sheepishly. "Yeah? Well, I told you it'd be big."

Maria stares at the crowd, gesturing at the sea of people filling the room. "Big? This is insane! We've never had this many people at once. The staff are starting to feel the strain. We prepared, but not for this kind of rush."

I can hear the hum of conversation growing louder and the crowd is definitely getting thicker, I can't help feeling a rush of pride. This is what we worked for. "Hey, the more people, the better, right? This means it's working. Jake's work is getting seen by everyone who matters."

Maria gives me a look, part amused, part exasperated. "Yeah, but if we can't keep things under control, this place is going to turn into chaos."

I chuckle, trying to keep it light. "It's art, Maria. A little chaos is part of the experience."

She rolls her eyes, yet her smile softens. "Well, you're definitely enjoying this, aren't you?"

"Okay, yeah," I admit, grinning. "Maybe a little. Seriously, this is what we wanted. More people means more eyes on Jake's work. It's only going to help him."

Maria sighs, glancing at the entrance as more guests pile in. "Fine, but we need to keep this organized. Can you make sure people aren't crowding too much near the entrance? I'll go check if we've got enough staff on hand. We might need to pull in more help."

I nod, scanning the room. "Yeah, I can handle that. I'll keep things flowing."

"Please," Maria says, her voice a bit more pleading now. "We just need to make sure no one freaks out in here."

I give her a quick thumbs-up. "Don't worry. I'll keep everyone in line. You go check on the staff and I'll make sure we don't have a riot."

She gives me a grateful smile, already turning to head toward the back. "Thanks. I'll be back in a few."

As Maria disappears into the crowd, I take a deep breath, glancing around at the guests, who are moving from one art piece to the next, some standing too long in one place, causing small bottlenecks. I step forward, gently guiding a few people to keep moving.

"Hey folks, feel free to keep walking around, there's a lot more to see," I say, smiling as politely as possible. "We've got plenty of room, no need to crowd in one spot."

A few guests nod and move along as I direct them and I quickly realize that while the rush is exciting, it's definitely pushing the limits of what we'd planned for. The staff at the front look frazzled, trying to manage the constant stream of guests coming in.

I walk over to the staff by the door. "How's it going?" I ask.

One of the greeters, a young guy with glasses, looks at me, his eyes wide. "We're good… it's just so many people. We weren't expecting this kind of turnout. I mean, we were expecting 300 people all day, not 300 in the first hour and a half."

"I know, I know," I say, patting him on the shoulder. "You're doing great. Just keep things moving and if you need help, let me know."

He nods, trying to muster a smile. "Thanks. We're managing, but I think we might need backup if this keeps up."

"I'll talk to Maria about getting more staff up here," I assure him. "In the meantime, just make sure people are moving through smoothly. Don't let anyone linger too long at the door."

As I turn back to face the crowd, I can't help feeling a little rush of adrenaline. This is exactly what we wanted—a packed exhibition, people excited and chatting about Jake's work. I also know we have to keep things from tipping over the edge into chaos.

I'm stationed at the reception desk, juggling guest lists and making sure the flow of people is moving as efficiently as possible. The exhibition is in full swing and the number of guests just keeps growing. Every now and then, I catch a glimpse of Jake in the distance, laughing and talking with a group of VIPs. He's in his element and the thought that this could be the start of something huge for him keeps me going, despite the craziness.

Just as I'm adjusting the list, I hear a familiar voice behind me.

"Well, well, if it isn't the man of the hour," Tess calls out, strolling up with Brody by his side.

I turn, grinning as I see them. "Hey, you guys made it!"

"Of course we did," Brody says, giving me a quick hug. "Wouldn't miss this for the world."

Tess looks around the bustling exhibition with wide eyes. "Man, this place is packed. You guys really pulled it off."

I laugh, shaking my head. "We're trying. It's pretty nuts, though."

"So, where's Jake?" Brody asks, glancing around. "We haven't seen him yet."

"He's giving a VIP tour to some important guests," I say, leaning in conspiratorially. "Big industry people. If they like what they see, Jake could be going international."

Tess whistles, clearly impressed. "No way. International? That's huge."

"Yeah," I say, feeling a surge of pride. "There are a few big wigs from the art world here. If they like Jake's work—and trust me, they will—he's gonna blow up. We're talking about galleries overseas, exhibits in major cities. The whole deal."

Brody raises an eyebrow, nodding thoughtfully. "Man, that's incredible. I mean, I always knew Jake was talented, but this? This is next-level."

Tess grins, nudging me with his elbow. "You and Maria have really put this thing on the map, huh?"

I shrug, unable to hide my grin. "It's been a team effort. Jake's the star, we just made sure everything was lined up right. Still, none of this would be happening if his work wasn't amazing."

Brody crosses his arms, taking in the scene. "It's wild to think about. Eight years ago he had moved back from UCLA, giving up his dreams of football just to draw a little. Now look at him."

I nod, looking over the crowd. "Yeah, it's kind of surreal."

Before I can say more, I spot Jamie walking in, looking around the room like she's scoping out the scene. I wave her over.

"Jamie!" I call. "Over here."

She makes her way through the crowd, a little smile on her face as she approaches us. "Hey, everything looks great."

"Yeah, it does," I say, quickly shifting into business mode. "But I need you to help out. The reception's getting swamped and we could use an extra set of hands."

Jamie raises an eyebrow, clearly not thrilled about the idea. "You want me to work the reception? Can't I just, like, enjoy the exhibition for a bit?"

I give her a pointed look, crossing my arms. "Nope. No time for that. We're drowning over here and you're not just here to wander around. Come on, lend a hand."

She sighs dramatically, rolling her eyes. "Fine, fine. I'll help."

Tess snickers, watching the exchange. "She's not gonna let you off easy, man."

I grin, already handing Jamie the guest list. "She never does."

Jamie shakes her head as she takes the list, standing next to me at the reception desk. "You owe me for this, Ethan."

I chuckle. "I'll owe you big time. Trust me, it'll be worth it."

Brody and Tess laugh, clearly entertained by the whole thing.

"So, what's next on the agenda, Mr. Manager?" Tess asks, folding his arms and leaning against the desk.

I glance at my phone, checking the schedule. "Next? We keep this crowd moving, make sure everyone's seen what they came for and keep the important people happy. If we pull this off, Jake's career is about to take off in a huge way."

Jamie leans over, scanning the crowd with me. "Well, let's make sure it doesn't go off the rails first."

I grin. "Exactly. Let's make it happen."

* * *

The reception desk is getting busier by the minute and I can already feel the tension building in the air. Things have been running smoothly for a while, then as if on cue, a small group of guests make their way to the counter, looking flustered and a little lost.

One of them, a middle-aged man in a suit, steps forward. "Excuse me, we're having some trouble figuring out where to go. The layout of the exhibition is a bit… confusing."

A woman beside him nods in agreement. "Yeah, we've been walking around and it's hard to tell where everything is. Do you have a map or something?"

I smile, trying to stay calm despite the growing crowd. "Sure thing. Let me grab one for you." I reach under the desk and pull out a map of the exhibition layout. "Here you go. This should help you navigate the different sections. There's a main hall here"—I point to the area marked—"then the smaller galleries are off to the side. The sculptures are in the far right wing."

The man squints at the map, looking it over. "Ah, I see now. That makes sense."

Another guest, a woman in a bright red dress, pipes up from behind him. "Also, we couldn't figure out where the refreshments were being served. Are they just in one spot?"

I nod. "Yeah, the refreshments are in the back corner of the gallery, near the exit. There's a small sign, I can see how it might be easy to miss with so many people here."

"Thanks," she says, smiling in relief. "We'll head there next."

Before I can take a breath, another guest, a man holding an empty water bottle, steps up to the counter with a frown. "Sorry, are there more water stations? It's getting pretty hot in there and the water seems to be running low."

I nod, feeling a bit of panic rising. "Yeah, I'll check on that for you. We've got a few water stations, however, I'll make sure someone refills them right away."

The man looks relieved. "Great, thanks. It's just a bit crowded and people are really thirsty."

"Got it. I'll make sure we sort it out." I shoot him a quick smile, then turn to Jamie, who's manning the guest list beside me.

"Hey, Jamie, can you radio the staff in the back? We need to get more water refills going ASAP."

Jamie nods, grabbing her walkie-talkie with a sigh. "On it. You're lucky I like you, Ethan."

I grin, even though the situation is starting to feel a little out of control. "You'd be lost without me, admit it."

Before Jamie can respond, another guest comes up, looking a bit frustrated. "Excuse me, I've been trying to find a particular piece of work— part of Jake's '*Everest at Home*' Collection. The place is so packed I couldn't figure out where it is on the map."

I point to the right wing of the gallery. "That particular piece is showcased in the main gallery on the right. Just head straight through the main hallway and you'll see a big sign for that collection. It's a bit crowded, but once you get there, you'll be able to find it easily."

The guest nods, except, I can tell from her expression that she's still feeling a little overwhelmed. "Okay, thanks. I'll give it another shot."

As soon as she leaves, Jamie turns to me with a raised eyebrow. "This is starting to feel like a madhouse."

I let out a deep breath. "Yeah, I know. I wasn't expecting so many people to have issues all at once."

Just then, another guest, a younger guy in a turtleneck, walks up with a puzzled look. "Uh, I'm having trouble figuring out where the interactive installation is. Is there a guide or something?"

I point to the far left corner of the gallery. "The interactive installation is in the far-left wing, past the photography exhibit. It's tucked away, so it's easy to miss, but once you're there, you'll know you're there, it get's pretty messy in there."

The guy nods. "Thanks, man. I've been wandering around for a while."

As soon as he leaves, Jamie lowers her voice and leans in toward me. "How are you keeping it together? I'm barely hanging on and I've only been here for like 20 minutes."

I give her a tired smile. "I'm pretending I'm not freaking out on the inside."

She laughs and it's the kind of laugh that says she totally understands. "Same."

Before I can respond, Maria appears from behind me, her brow furrowed in concern. "Ethan, I heard there are issues with the refreshments?"

"Yeah," I say quickly, glancing at the growing line of guests behind the counter. "People are saying the water stations are running low. I asked Jamie to radio the staff to refill them."

Maria nods, already on her phone. "I'll get it handled. Keep the guests calm. We don't need a riot over water."

"Working on it," I say, trying to keep my voice steady.

As Maria rushes off, I turn back to the guests. Another group has approached the counter, looking confused about where to go next. I take a deep breath, forcing a smile.

"Hi, folks. How can I help you?"

* * *

The exhibition is in full swing and after what feels like a hundred questions about the layout and the refreshments, I'm back at the reception desk, directing people like a human GPS. I can feel myself fading, quickly. I haven't eaten since dinner last night and I've barely had time to drink anything, but I keep smiling and giving instructions.

"Bathrooms are down the hall to your left," I say for what feels like the thousandth time, pointing to yet another confused guest.

Out of the corner of my eye, I see Jake returning from his VIP tour. He looks pumped, like the tour has gone perfectly. He makes his way over to the desk, flashing his signature grin. "Hey, I'm back. You good? Any other guests who need the VIP treatment?"

I sigh, rubbing the back of my neck. "Yeah, sure, if by VIP treatment you mean a tour to the bathroom. Can you handle that?" I add, half-joking, but my tone has an edge of exhaustion.

Jake blinks, clearly confused. "Wait... what? Tour to the bathroom?"

I laugh, though it comes out more sarcastic than I intend. "Yeah, that's pretty much what it feels like right now. I've been sitting here giving directions non-stop. You know, to the bathrooms, water stations, exits—real glamorous stuff."

Jake raises an eyebrow and glances down at the guest list in front of me. It's a complete disaster—names crossed out, notes scribbled all over the place and sticky notes everywhere. I don't even want to look at it anymore.

"Whoa, what's going on here?" Jake asks, frowning as he tries to make sense of the chaos on the desk.

I throw my hands up, feeling the frustration finally bubbling over. "What's happening? What's happening is that we have a staff issue. We've got way more people than we expected, the team can't keep up. It's a mess, Jake. People keep getting confused and no one's managing the flow properly."

Jake looks at me, his brows furrowed, clearly trying to stay calm. "Alright, I get it. It's crazy, but we'll figure it out. Let's get the staff—"

"Figure it out?" I interrupt, my voice more hostile than I wanted it to be. "Jake, I've been 'figuring it out' for hours! I've been running around trying to keep this thing together while you've been off giving tours to VIPs. I'm exhausted. We don't have enough staff and people are getting irritated. It's getting out of control."

Jake's face softens a bit, but he doesn't back down. "Look, I know it's a lot and I didn't mean to leave you hanging. We're a team. Let's tackle this together, okay? I'll handle the next round of guests—"

I cut him off again, standing up from behind the counter. "You don't get it, Jake. It's not just about handling the guests. It's the logistics, the water stations running dry, the confusion about where to go... I've been doing everything I can, it's just overwhelming. We didn't plan for anything this crazy."

Jake steps closer, trying to meet my gaze. "Ethan, I'm not trying to make things harder for you. I just—"

"I need to get some air," I mutter, my voice barely above a whisper, however, I can't stop the frustration from leaking out. "I just... need a break."

Before Jake can respond, I push past him, heading for the exit. The noise of the exhibition fades as I step outside into the crisp air. I lean against the wall, closing my eyes and taking a deep breath.

I know Jake isn't trying to push me, everything just piled up so quickly. I'm not even mad at him—I'm mad at the whole situation, at how chaotic everything has become. I just need a moment to breathe.

fourteen

I sit on a bench in the park, staring out at nothing in particular. The place is full of life—kids running around, playing tag, laughing without a care in the world. I can hear the distant chirping of birds fluttering between the trees and a light breeze rustles the leaves overhead. But none of it registers. None of it feels real. Not to me, anyway.

All I can think about is how badly I've screwed things up. I shouldn't have snapped at Jake. He didn't deserve that. He was doing what he had to, managing the VIPs, keeping the big names happy. It wasn't his fault that everything at the reception desk spiraled out of control. Yet, I dumped all my frustration on him like it was.

"Idiot," I mutter under my breath, rubbing my temples as if that will somehow erase the memory of me walking out on him. What was I thinking? Jake came to help and instead of letting him, I pushed him away. Typical.

I lean forward, resting my elbows on my knees and staring down at the ground. The gravel underfoot seems more interesting than the vibrant world around me. *Why did I do that? Why do I always do that?*

It wasn't even Jake I was angry with. It was everything else. The exhibition, the guests, the chaos of it all. It built up until I couldn't handle it anymore and Jake just happened to be standing there when it all exploded. I know that doesn't make it right. I should've kept my cool. I should've talked to him instead of snapping.

I close my eyes and let out a long sigh. "Too late now."

The kids' laughter echoes across the park and for a moment, I let myself focus on that. It's strange how life just keeps moving, no matter what kind of mess you're dealing with. The world doesn't stop for your problems. Birds keep chirping, kids keep playing, and the sky still stretches on, no matter how heavy your heart feels.

"Get over it," I whisper to myself, yet it doesn't help. I can't just shrug it off. Jake is the person I'm closest to right now and I lashed out at him when he didn't deserve it. Now I'm sitting here, stewing in my own guilt, while he's probably still at the exhibition, trying to keep everything together without me.

I run my hand through my hair, frustrated with myself. *I should go back*, I think to myself, though I stay rooted to the bench. Part of me doesn't want to face him. I don't want to see the look on his face—the disappointment I know will be there.

What am I supposed to do? Sit here in the park and hide from it all? That's not going to fix anything. Jake will forgive me, I know that. He's not the type to hold a grudge, even if that doesn't make the guilt any easier to swallow.

"I should've handled it better," I whisper again, more to myself than anything. "But there's no going back now, is there?"

The wind picks up, rustling the leaves in the trees. My mind is stuck in a loop, replaying the moment over and over. Jake standing there, confused, trying to understand why I was so upset. And me, walking out like a fool.

"God, I'm such an idiot," I groan, burying my face in my hands.

I don't know how long I've been sitting here, it feels like hours. I glance up at the kids again, running across the snow-covered grass, carefree and light. A part of me envies them. They don't have to deal with the weight of screwing up a friendship, of letting someone down when they need you the most.

I'm still sitting on the park bench, trying to wrap my head around everything, when I hear footsteps pounding on the pavement behind me. At first, I don't think much of it—probably just some jogger— then I hear my name.

"Ethan!"

I turn around and there's Jake, sprinting toward me, looking out of breath. His face is a mix of relief and concern, but also something else—something that makes me feel even worse about leaving the exhibition in the first place.

"Jake?" I stand up, genuinely surprised to see him. "What are you doing here? You should be at the exhibition."

He stops right in front of me, hands on his knees as he catches his breath. "I… I had to come find you," he says between breaths. "I couldn't just let you leave like that."

I frown, shaking my head. "Jake, seriously, I'm fine. You didn't have to—"

"No," Jake cuts me off, standing up straight now. "I do have to. I screwed up. I didn't see how much you were handling on your own back there and I'm sorry. I should've been helping, instead, I was off doing the easy stuff while you were dealing with all the chaos."

I open my mouth to respond, but he keeps going.

"Maria told me how hard things have been at the reception," Jake continues, his voice full of guilt. "I didn't get it at first, but now I do. You were running everything and I wasn't there to back you up. I shouldn't have left you to deal with all that by yourself."

I sigh, running a hand through my hair. "Jake, it's not a big deal. You were handling the VIPs. That's what we planned for. I just… I got overwhelmed, that's all."

Jake shakes his head, stepping closer. "No, Ethan. It is a big deal. You've been holding this whole exhibition together and I took it for granted. I was so focused on impressing the VIPs that I didn't even realize how much pressure I was putting on you."

I look at him, trying to find the right words. "Jake, I'm not mad. I was just frustrated. Everything hit at once and I didn't handle it well. That's on me, not you. I'm sorry for snapping at you."

He shakes his head again, more firmly this time. "No, babe. You've done everything for this exhibition—everything. And if you're not there, it doesn't matter how many people show up or how many VIPs I impress. If you're not part of it, what's the point?"

I stare at him for a moment, feeling the weight of his words sink in. He called me 'babe.' Jake isn't just saying this to make me feel better—he genuinely means it. He's not the kind of guy to throw around empty words and hearing him say that makes the knot in my chest loosen just a little.

"Jake, it's not like that," I say softly. "The exhibition is about your work."

He steps even closer, his voice quieter now. "This isn't just my exhibition, Ethan. This whole thing wouldn't be happening without you. You're the reason this exhibition even got off the ground. I couldn't have done it without you and I don't want to keep doing it without you."

I look down at my feet, feeling the guilt creeping back in. "I didn't mean to walk out like that. I just... I needed to clear my head. It was too much all at once."

"I get that," Jake says, his tone understanding. "I really do. And I'm sorry if I made you feel like you had to do it all on your own."

For a moment, we stand there in silence, the noise of the park fading into the background. The breeze rustles the empty branches overhead and I can hear the distant laughter of the kids playing, yet all I can focus on is Jake standing in front of me, his eyes full of sincerity.

Finally, I let out a deep breath and nod. "Okay. Let's go back. There's still a ton of people at the exhibition and we've got a lot to manage."

Jake smiles, except it's not his usual playful grin —it's something more tender, more genuine. "Yeah, let's do that. Only if you're good with it."

I give him a small smile. "I'm good. I just needed a breather. Now I'm ready to jump back in."

Jake claps me on the shoulder. "Alright, let's finish what we started. Together."

* * *

I stand off to the side, watching as the exhibition runs without a problem. While the chaos from earlier in the day still lingers in my mind, things feel a lot calmer. Maria is running around, making sure everything is in order and Jake has just finished chatting with a few important guests. I can see the excitement in his eyes as he makes his way toward the small stage at the front of the gallery.

He turns to me, giving me a quick smile, then steps up to the microphone, tapping it gently to get everyone's attention. The murmur of conversation slowly dies down and the guests turn their focus to Jake, who stands there looking as calm and collected as ever.

"Good evening, everyone!" Jake calls out, his voice booming through the space with that easy confidence of his. "First of all, I want to thank each and every one of you for being here this evening, on the second day of this exhibition. It means the world to me to see so many familiar faces, as well as some new ones."

The room fills with polite applause and I can't help smiling at the sight of Jake up there, completely owning the moment.

Jake holds up his hands, signaling for the applause to quiet down. "I also want to take a moment to apologize for any inconvenience you may have had earlier today. We had a lot more people show up than expected and things got a little hectic." He chuckles and a few guests laugh along with him. "But hey, that's what happens when you're lucky enough to have so many people interested in what you're doing, right?"

More laughter follows and the tension in the room seems to lift even further. Jake has this way of making people feel like everything is under control, even when it isn't.

"Now, none of this would've been possible without a few very special people," Jake continues, his tone soothing. "First, I want to thank Maria, who has been by my side for the last eight years, organizing every exhibition, keeping me sane and making sure that I don't completely lose it during times like these."

He turns toward Maria who is standing in the crowd with a smile on her face. The room erupts into applause again and Maria gives a modest wave. Jake grins. "Seriously, without her, this exhibition would be a total mess. So, thank you, Maria. You're the best."

The clapping dies down again and then Jake's eyes scan the room until they land on me. For a second, my stomach drops. I know what's coming, but it doesn't stop the nerves from creeping in.

"And also," Jake says, his voice growing even more sincere, "there's someone else who made this exhibition possible—someone who has been working tirelessly behind the scenes, making sure everything went off without a hitch, even when things were falling apart. Without this person, none of what you see today would've happened."

My heart races as he looks directly at me.

"Ladies and gentlemen," Jake continues, motioning towards me, "I want to introduce you to the man who's been the backbone of this entire exhibition: Ethan."

The crowd erupts into cheers and applause and I feel my face flush as I realize everyone is looking at me. I'm never one for the spotlight, but here I am, with dozens of eyes on me.

Jake gestures for me to come up to the front and I hesitate for a second before taking a deep breath and walking toward him. As I make my way through the crowd, I see people clapping and smiling at me. I realize for the first time in what feels like forever, I don't feel overwhelmed. I feel... proud.

I step up to the small stage and stand beside Jake, who wraps an arm around my shoulder, pulling me into a quick, playful hug. "This guy," Jake says into the microphone, grinning from ear to ear, "is the reason I still have hair on my head. He's been keeping everything functional, even when I was off doing my VIP thing."

The crowd laughs and I can't help letting out a chuckle too, even as I feel my nerves still buzzing under the surface.

Jake turns toward me, speaking quieter now, still into the mic. "Seriously, Ethan. Thank you. I couldn't have done this without you."

I glance at him, feeling a lump in my throat. "Hey, it's nothing. You're the one with the talent. I only organized things to bring people in."

Jake shakes his head, still smiling. "It's not just about that. You were the one holding everything together. I mean it."

The crowd is still clapping and I glance out to see Jamie standing by the reception desk. She's been irritated all day, dealing with the chaos and the work, but now, for the first time, I see her smile. She catches my eye and gives me a thumbs-up, the relief clear on her face. Seeing her like that makes the moment even better.

Jake leans into the mic again. "Alright, let's get back to enjoying the exhibition, shall we? Thank you all again for being here. This exhibition is for all of you."

As the applause fills the room again, Jake gives me another squeeze on the shoulder before stepping back. I stay beside him for a moment, still processing the cheers, the clapping, the sheer joy from everyone around us.

fifteen

I walk into the exhibition space early on the final day, determined to make sure everything goes according to plan. The previous days have been a rollercoaster of stress and stimulation, but now that we're nearing the end, I can finally see the finish line. The gallery is quiet, with only a few staff members moving around, preparing for the crowds that will arrive soon.

Maria, as usual, is already hard at work. She's off to the side, talking to a group of new staffers, showing them the ropes. When she sees me walk in, a look of relief crosses her face.

"Ethan! Thank God you're here," she says, waving me over.

I smile, already bracing myself for whatever she's got in store. "Hey, Maria. How's it going? Everything under control?"

She hands me a clipboard with the day's guest list, her eyes serious as she focuses on me. "For the most part, yes. But we've got a curveball."

I raise an eyebrow, flipping through the list. "Curveball?"

"Yeah," she says, lowering her voice a little. "Senator Michael Alfort might be coming today."

I stop mid-flip, staring at her. "Wait, what? Senator Alfort? As in *the* Senator Alfort?"

Maria nods, her expression calm but intense. "Yeah. I got the heads-up this morning. Apparently, one of his people reached out. He's interested in checking out the exhibition."

I blink, trying to process what she's saying. "That's huge. I mean, the guy's one of the most high-profile people in the state. Why is he coming here?"

Maria shrugs. "Word must've gotten around. We've had some serious social media coverage over the past couple of days, especially with some of the VIPs who've already been here. Jake's work is catching the right eyes and apparently, Alfort's one of them."

I stand there, still processing the weight of what she's just dropped on me. Senator Michael Alfort isn't just any guest. He's a major political figure, someone who could bring a level of attention and scrutiny we aren't exactly prepared for.

"Okay," I say slowly, flipping back to the guest list. "So… what do we do if he shows up? How do we handle this?"

Maria smirks, clearly amused by how thrown I am. "Relax. We've handled big names before. It's just that this one's a little bigger. We'll treat him like any other VIP, but we need to be sharp. No slip-ups, no disorganization."

I nod, my mind already spinning with the logistics. "Right. Sharp. Got it. Why didn't we know about this earlier?"

Maria sighs. "I only got the note this morning. It wasn't a sure thing until now. I'm guessing he's a last-minute kind of guy."

"Great," I mutter, rubbing my forehead. "Just what we needed on the final day—a senator with a surprise appearance."

Maria gives me a reassuring smile. "Ethan, we can do this. Because Jake needs us to."

I take a deep breath, mentally running through everything I'll need to do. "You're right, we've got this. This is what we all wanted at the start of all of this; to get Jake noticed. Well, this will get him noticed for sure!"

"I know you can do it," Maria says, giving me a pat on the shoulder. "Besides, I'll be around to help. We've got extra staff today, so you won't be juggling everything by yourself."

I glance over at the group of new staffers Maria's been instructing. They look eager, but also slightly overwhelmed. I can relate.

"Are the new staff ready?" I ask, gesturing toward them. "I mean, if Alfort shows up, they're going to need to be on point."

"They'll be fine," Maria assures me. "I've given them the rundown and they know what's expected. We've got this covered."

I nod, trying to push away the nerves. "Okay. And Jake? Does he know about this?"

Maria rolls her eyes playfully. "Not yet. I figured I'd let you tell him once he's finished with his morning meditation or whatever he's doing. We wouldn't want to throw him off his zen."

I laugh, feeling a little more relaxed. "Right. We wouldn't want to disrupt the artist's process."

"Exactly," Maria says with a smirk. "Seriously, Ethan, we'll be fine. You've done an incredible job so far and this is just another challenge. I have no doubt we can handle it."

I look down at the guest list one more time, scanning for any other surprises, but Senator Alfort's name is the only one sending my heart racing. "Alright," I say, exhaling deeply. "Let's make this last day count."

Maria gives me a confident nod. "We will. And hey, who knows? Maybe having a senator at Jake's exhibition will be the kind of boost we didn't even know we needed."

I grin, feeling the tension start to lift. "Let's hope so."

* * *

The exhibition is finally open and running without any of the chaos that had plagued the past few days. The once palpable tension is now replaced by a steady hum of excitement as guests move through the space, admiring Jake's work. I stand by the entrance, clipboard in hand, taking a moment to breathe and enjoy the brief calm before the next wave of visitors arrives.

I glance up from my checklist and spot Jake across the room. He's pacing near one of his larger canvases, speaking with a couple of attendees, but there's a tightness in his movements. Even from here, I can tell he's nervous—probably more than he's letting on. His usual confidence, the way he effortlessly captivates people with his art, is missing.

I make my way over to him, weaving through the crowd and by the time I reach him, the guests he's speaking with have already moved on.

"Jake!" I call out over the bustle of the surrounding crowd. "Do you have a quick second?"

He turns toward me, a warm smile lighting up his face. "Of course, anything for you," Jake says, grabbing my forearm and pulling me to a quieter corner away from the patrons and noise.

"What's up?" he asks, his tone still light, though I can sense the undercurrent of tension from the busy day.

I take a deep breath, trying to find the best way to deliver the news without sending him into a panic. "Okay, I don't want you to freak out," I say, placing my hands on his shoulders, hoping to steady him. "But… Senator Alfort is rumored to be making an appearance today."

Jake's expression doesn't falter, not even for a second. He chuckles softly, shrugging as if I'd just told him we were out of napkins. "Really? The senator? That's… cool, I guess," he says, his voice calm, almost dismissive. "No big deal."

I blink, surprised by how laid-back he seems. "No big deal?" I repeat, narrowing my eyes at him. "Jake, this is *huge*. The guy's one of the most high-profile people in the state. If he likes your work, this could open doors for you that you can't even imagine."

Jake shrugs again, keeping his tone casual. "Yeah, I get that. It's just another person, right? If he shows up, he shows up. I'm not going to stress about it." He gives me a reassuring smile, as if he's completely unfazed.

I nod slowly, not quite buying the cool exterior, but deciding to go along with it. "Okay… if you're sure. I just thought you'd want to know."

He claps me on the shoulder, that easy grin still plastered on his face. "I appreciate the heads-up, Ethan. I'm good. I've handled high-profile people before."

I smile, relieved that he's not freaking out—at least, not outwardly. "Alright, well, just let me know if you need anything. I'll be around."

Jake nods, the casual facade still perfectly in place. "Thanks, man. I've got this."

As I turn to walk away, I glance back at him, just in time to catch a brief flicker of something in his eyes—a flash of uncertainty, maybe even anxiety. It's gone as quickly as it appeared, replaced by that same calm, collected look. But now, I'm starting to wonder if Jake's coolness is all just a front.

Still, I leave him to it, thinking maybe he just needs a minute to collect himself. He's got this—he *always* does.

What I don't see, though, as I walk away, is the way Jake takes a deep breath, running a hand through his hair as he stares down at the floor for a long moment, his foot tapping nervously.

* * *

"Hey, Maria," I call out, walking over to where she's checking on the staff. "Where's Jake? I can't find him and the Senator just walked in."

Maria looks up from her clipboard, her expression lightening slightly. "He's been busy."

I frown. "Busy with what?"

She sighs and lowers her clipboard. "He's been meeting with a bunch of new clients—some big names who've shown serious interest in his work. He's already sold a good chunk of his paintings."

I blink, surprised. "Wait, already? That's amazing."

"Yeah," Maria nods, though her face doesn't exactly light up with joy. "It is. He's made some solid connections too. A few collectors, gallery owners, even some folks from out of the country."

I smile, but something in Maria's tone makes me pause. "That sounds great. So… why do you look like it's not?"

She glances around, making sure no one is within earshot before stepping a little closer. "Look, it is great. Jake's been killing it. However, he's also stressed."

"Stressed? About what?" I ask, confused. "He's selling his paintings, making connections—he should be over the moon right now."

Maria bites her lip, then sighs. "I told him that, he's just feeling like there's a lot of pressure. Especially with the possibility of the senator showing up and by what you just said, he's already here. He's been going back and forth about whether or not he should even try to sell something to Senator Alfort."

I raise an eyebrow. "Why would he be stressed about that? If Alfort buys one of his pieces, that's a huge win."

"I know," Maria says, nodding, "Jake's... well, you know how he gets. He's overthinking it. He's worried that if he pushes too hard, it'll come off as desperate and if he doesn't push at all, he'll lose out on a major opportunity. Plus, selling to someone as high-profile as a senator comes with all kinds of expectations."

I shake my head, trying to make sense of it. "This is exactly what we've been working toward, right? Getting his work in front of the right people. I don't get why he's second-guessing himself now."

Maria sighs, crossing her arms. "Because it's Jake. He's an artist, not a salesman. The thing is, he cares about his work—really cares. It's not just about making a sale for him. He wants to make sure that whoever buys his paintings understands them, respects them. He's afraid that selling to someone like Alfort could mean compromising that."

I let out a slow breath, understanding now why Jake hasn't shown up. He's caught in his own head, overanalyzing every move. It's classic Jake, really brilliant, but always worried about doing the right thing by his art.

"Okay, so what do we do?" I ask, leaning against the wall. "I can't let him spiral like this, especially today. He's been doing amazing."

Maria nods. "I know. Honestly, I think he just needs a nudge. You seem to be the only one who can get through to him when he's like this."

I raise an eyebrow. "Me?"

"Yeah," she says, giving me a knowing smile. "You're the one to calm him down when he gets in his own way. You know how to remind him what really matters."

I sigh, running a hand through my hair. "Right. So, where is he now?"

Maria gestures toward the back of the gallery. "Last I saw, he was with a couple of clients near the private viewing area. He might still be there."

I nod. "Okay. I'll go talk to him. He's got no reason to be stressed about this. I'll make sure he knows that."

I survey the exhibition and see Jake walking into the back storage room alone. I gesture to Maria that I'll be right back and follow Jake.

"Hey," I say gently, giving him a reassuring smile. "How are you holding up?"

He sighs, rubbing the back of his neck. "Honestly? I feel like I'm about to lose it."

I nod, stepping closer. "What's going on? Everything seems to be running smoothly."

Jake lets out a quiet laugh, though it's strained. "Yeah, from the outside, maybe. But inside, I'm a mess. I can't stop thinking about the senator. I don't know what to do, Ethan. If I sell something to him... I don't know if that's the right move."

I frown, sensing the weight of the decision pressing on him. "You're worried about selling to someone like Alfort?"

Jake nods, his brow furrowing. "It's not just selling to him, though. It's what comes with it. The expectations. The scrutiny. What if he doesn't actually get what I'm trying to say with my work? What if it's just a status thing for him? I don't want my art to be... commodified like that."

I place a reassuring hand on his arm, giving it a gentle squeeze. "Jake, I get it. But you can't let that kind of pressure ruin this moment for you. You've worked hard for this. Whether or not you sell to Alfort doesn't define who you are as an artist. It's just one buyer."

He looks at me, his eyes searching mine, clearly still conflicted. "It's not just any buyer. A senator? That's not something you just ignore."

"I know," I reply, my voice calm. "Remember, he's just one person. He doesn't get to define your work. You do. You get to decide who you sell to and how you want your art to be seen. If you feel like selling to him would compromise what your work means to you, then don't do it. If you think it's an opportunity to put your art in front of someone who can amplify your message, then maybe it's worth considering."

Jake chews on his bottom lip, looking down at the floor. "I just don't want to make the wrong choice."

I smile, nudging him lightly with my elbow. "There's no wrong choice here, Jake. You're in control. You know what feels right."

He meets my gaze, the tension in his shoulders easing just a little. "You always know how to calm me down."

I chuckle quietly. "That's what I'm here for."

For a moment, we just stand there, the noise of the exhibition fading into the background. The closeness between us feels comforting, like a quiet understanding that doesn't need words.

I open the door to lead Jake to the senator, and just as I do, I spot Maria heading toward us. She's weaving through the guests, looking far more relaxed than she's been the past few days. Her usual no-nonsense expression is replaced by a small, almost relieved smile.

"Hey, Ethan. Jake," she says, nodding at both of us as she reaches us. "Things are running efficiently. I have to say, it's going a lot better than I expected."

I give her a smile. "That's because you're a master at this, Maria."

She chuckles, shaking her head. "It's more that Jake's work is getting a lot of attention. People are really responding to it."

Jake glances between us, a faint smile tugging at his lips. "I'm just trying not to let it all get to me."

Maria gives him a reassuring nod. "You're doing great. Just keep going. This is your moment."

Jake looks at me again and I can see the gratitude in his eyes. He still looks a little uncertain, but the anxiety that was eating away at him moments ago has faded.

"Thanks, Ethan," he says quietly, almost as if it's just for me. "I needed that."

I smile, feeling the heartfelt moment between us. "Anytime."

Before we can say more, a new wave of guests starts to arrive and the calm of the moment dissolves as we dive back into the flow of the exhibition. I can see the difference in Jake's posture now—he's more grounded, more sure of himself. And I can't help but feel a little proud that I was able to help him find his balance again.

"Hey, Ethan," Maria stops me as I'm about to walk back toward the front doors. "Got a minute?"

I glance around, making sure everything is under control, then walk over to her. "Yeah, what's up? Things seem to be under control for once."

Maria smiles, tilting her head toward the exit. "Come on, let's grab a coffee. You've been running around like a maniac and I think we both deserve a break."

I hesitate for a second, thinking about all the things I still need to check, but then I nod. "Alright, coffee sounds good. I could use a break before the next wave of people and by the looks of it, Jake is meeting with the senator right now, so we should be in the clear."

We make our way out of the gallery and across the street to a small café. It's one of those cozy spots with low lighting and quiet jazz playing in the background. When we step inside, I feel myself relax a little. We grab our coffees and sit by the window, the exhibition visible just across the street.

Maria stirs her coffee for a moment and I can tell something is on her mind. She's usually a little neurotic, but today she seems... different. I wait for her to say something, so when she doesn't, I finally speak up.

"So, what's up? You've got that look like there's something you want to talk about," I say, raising an eyebrow.

Maria glances at me, her expression thoughtful. "Yeah, there is. I've been thinking about something for a while and I figured I should just tell you."

I take a sip of my coffee, leaning back in my chair. "Okay... I'm listening."

She hesitates for a second, then sighs. "I like Jake."

I freeze, nearly choking on my coffee. "Wait, what?" I set my cup down, staring at her in surprise. "You mean… like him more than a friend?"

Maria nods, looking out the window. "Yeah, I do. I've liked him for a while now."

My mind races. This is not what I expected her to say. Maria and Jake are close, but I thought it was more of a professional relationship—a partnership, almost. "I had no idea," I mutter, still trying to wrap my head around it.

Maria chuckles, though there's a hint of sadness in her voice. "Yeah, well, I didn't expect you to know. I haven't exactly been open about it."

I rub the back of my neck, feeling a bit of awkwardness creeping in. "Does Jake know?"

She shakes her head. "No, I don't think so. We're good friends, however, I don't think he has any interest in me… not like that, anyway."

I frown, trying to piece it all together. "Well, you know how Jake can be sometimes. Oblivious to everything except for art."

She sighs, her fingers tracing the rim of her coffee cup. "Well, I just wanted to tell you because I've been watching you and Jake. The way you two are around each other, it's different. And I don't want there to be any weirdness between us. I know how close you two are."

I stare at her for a second, my mind spinning. "What do you mean? We're just friends." I lie. I feel like we're more than friends, I just don't know if that's what Jake wants, especially since I'll be going back to the city soon. "We've been through a lot together and I'm helping him with the exhibition. That's it."

Maria gives me a small smile, though there's something knowing in her expression. "Maybe. Still, you and I both know there's more to it than that. You care about him and I know he cares about you."

I open my mouth to argue, only to close it again. The truth is, I do care about Jake—more than I want to admit. I'm just not ready to say that out loud—not to Maria and definitely not to myself.

"I just thought it was fair to tell you," Maria continues, breaking the silence. "Even though I know Jake's probably not interested in me that way, I can't ignore my feelings. I don't want this to become some weird thing between us. I value our friendship, Ethan. And I know how important Jake is to you."

I sit there, unsure of how to respond. Part of me wants to tell her she's wrong, that I'm not feeling anything more than friendship for Jake. But another part of me—the part I've been avoiding for a while now—knows there's more to it.

"Why now?" I ask again, my voice gentler this time.

Maria looks down at her coffee for a moment before answering. "Because I wanted you to know before things got complicated. I've seen the way Jake looks at you when you're not paying attention. You're important to him, Ethan. I just need you to know that he's important to me too."

Her words hit me like a punch to the gut. I haven't noticed anything about the way Jake looks at me—have I? It feels like the ground beneath me is shifting and I'm not sure what to do with that.

I finally let out a shaky breath. "Maria, I don't even know what to say."

"You don't have to say anything," she replies gently. "I'm not telling you this to make things harder. I just thought you should know where I stand. Whatever happens, I'm still going to be here. And Jake will be too."

I nod slowly, trying to process it all. "Thanks for telling me. I guess I… needed to hear it."

sixteen

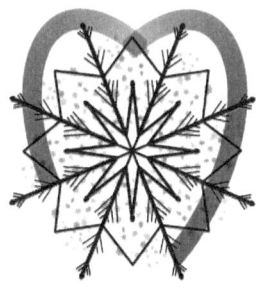

Maria's words keep replaying in my head as I walk back to the exhibition, each step feeling heavier than the last. *I like Jake.* It echoes over and over, refusing to leave my mind. Jake and I aren't together—not officially. Not in any way that matters on paper, at least. Hearing Maria confess that she likes him, that she hasn't given up on the idea of being with him, makes something twist deep in my chest.

Why does it bother me so much?

I try to shake off the feeling as I step back into the gallery, but my heart is still in turmoil. The thought of Jake with someone else—with Maria—makes something in me ache. Maybe it's the fact that Maria is so calm, so sure of her feelings, while I'm still stumbling through mine. Whatever it is, it leaves a weight on my heart.

When I enter the exhibition space, everything is running like clockwork. The staff manages the guests, the art is being admired and the atmosphere crackles with adrenaline. It's exactly how we had hoped the final day would be. I spot Jake at the front of the room, standing near the stage and as soon as he catches sight of me, he motions for me to come over.

I take a deep breath, pushing aside the whirlwind of thoughts and walk toward him. Jake grabs the mic and taps it, drawing the room's attention. He looks as composed as ever, self-assurance radiating through the room as he prepares to speak.

"Hey, everyone," Jake says, his voice fearless and full of energy. "First, I just want to thank all of you for being here and making this exhibition such a success. It's been an incredible journey and I couldn't have done it without your support."

There's a round of applause and Jake smiles, pausing for a moment before continuing. "Now, to celebrate the success of the exhibition, I'd like to invite everyone to a little New Year's Eve party this evening hosted by my good friend Tess at his café. We'll have drinks, music, and a chance to unwind after what's been an amazing few days."

Another wave of applause as Jake nods, clearly pleased with the response. I watch him as he speaks, feeling that familiar flutter in my chest—mixed now with a strange sense of unease after Maria's confession.

After addressing the crowd, Jake steps off the small stage and approaches me. His usual easy smile remains, though his eyes narrow slightly as he senses something is off.

"Hey," he says, his hand slowly and gently touching mine. "Everything good?"

I force a smile, trying to keep my voice steady. "Yeah, everything's under control. The guests are all set."

Jake nods, his smile relaxing. "Good. I knew I could count on you." He pauses for a second, his eyes searching mine. "You sure you're okay? You look a little… distracted."

I shrug, not wanting to get into it right now. "Just a lot on my mind, I guess. It's nothing serious."

Jake watches me for a moment longer, his expression thoughtful, before letting it go. "Alright, if you say so. Anyway, I've got something to ask you."

"What's up?" I ask, grateful for the distraction.

"Are you free for the next couple of hours?" Jake asks casually, though there's a hint of something in his tone that makes me pause.

I glance around, making sure the staff has everything under control. "Yeah, everything's been handled with the guests. I'm free."

Jake's grin widens and he leans in a little. "Good. Be ready in thirty minutes. I'm taking you out for lunch."

I blink in surprise. "Lunch? Now?"

"Yeah," he says, still smiling. "You've been running around like crazy all weekend and I figured it's about time we took a break. Besides, I want to talk to you about something."

My heart does a strange little flip. "Talk to me? About what?"

Jake shrugs, but there's that same playful glint in his eyes that always puts me at ease. "You'll see. Just be ready, alright?"

I watch him for a moment, my mind racing. After everything Maria said, after the confusing mess of emotions swirling around inside me, the last thing I expect is for Jake to invite me out for lunch, yet here he is, looking at me like nothing has changed, like it's the most natural thing in the world.

"Alright," I say finally, nodding. "I'll be ready in thirty."

Jake gives my hand a quick squeeze. "Perfect. I'll meet you out front with my car."

* * *

I stand outside the exhibition, shifting from foot to foot, checking the time on my phone for what feels like the hundredth time. The day is warmer than expected, so I left my coat behind, feeling the soft touch of sunlight on my back. I'm dressed in a black button-down and gray jeans—casual but decent enough for lunch, or at least I hope it is.

Jake's been vague about the details, which only makes me more anxious.

I sigh, running a hand through my hair just as I hear the low rumble of an engine. Looking up, I spot Jake's car rolling down the street. He pulls up in front of me, dressed in a simple black T-shirt and white trousers, yet somehow, he looks effortlessly put together. It's ridiculous how good he makes something so basic look.

He leans over, grinning from the driver's seat. "Hop in, handsome. You ready?"

I nod, my heart doing that strange flip again. "Yeah, I'm ready," I say as I head toward the car.

"Is it just us, or are the others coming too?" I ask, reaching for the door handle.

Jake tilts his head slightly, that playful smile tugging at the corners of his lips. "Just us. Thought we could use some time to catch up without everyone else from the exhibition hanging around."

His words send a little flutter through my stomach. I hadn't expected it to be just the two of us—especially not during his big weekend. "Oh," I reply, trying to keep my tone casual as I climb into the car. "Okay, cool."

Jake smirks, as if he knows exactly what I'm thinking. "Relax, Ethan. It's just lunch. Nothing too fancy."

I laugh nervously, shutting the door. "Right, lunch. Got it."

As soon as I'm buckled in, Jake shifts into gear, and we pull away from the exhibition. The city blurs past us as we drive, and I keep sneaking glances at him. He seems... different today. Lighter, more relaxed, as though the weight of the exhibition has melted away, leaving behind the Jake I knew before all this started—the Jake that feels like home.

"So," I start, breaking the comfortable silence, "where are we going?"

Jake keeps his eyes on the road, but I catch the small grin forming on his lips. "It's a surprise."

I raise an eyebrow, intrigued but also a little suspicious. "A surprise, huh? No hints at all?"

"Not a chance," he says, his grin widening. "You'll find out soon enough. Trust me, you're gonna love it."

I let out a small laugh, shaking my head. "You and your surprises."

"Hey, I gotta keep things interesting—like you and that snowball you threw at me the other day," Jake says, glancing at me for a second before returning his focus to the road. "Besides, you've been working like crazy these past few days. You deserve a break."

I can't help the smile that comes from him saying that, even though my mind is still racing with everything Maria said earlier. *Does he know? Does he feel the same way?* I don't know how to bring it up—or even if I should. Being in the car with him, just the two of us, feels… special. It's not like our usual banter or casual hangouts. Something is shifting, and I'm both terrified and ecstatic.

As we drive in comfortable silence, I lean back in my seat and watch Everest fade into the distance. My thoughts are still tangled up, but for now, I decide to just go with it. Whatever is happening between us, whatever this lunch is about, I'll deal with it when the moment comes.

We've been driving for what feels like ages. First, it's smooth sailing on the highway—Jake keeping the conversation light, cracking jokes, and teasing me about how tense I am—then we hit a dirt trail. That's when I start getting curious. The town is long behind us and the vibe has shifted. There are no more Christmas lights or friendly faces, just open fields and tall trees.

The car bounces a bit as Jake navigates the uneven trail, the tires kicking up muddy snow behind us. I glance over at him, raising an eyebrow. "You sure we're not getting lost out here? Feels like the middle of nowhere."

Jake just chuckles, his hands steady on the wheel. "Trust me, Ethan. I know where I'm going."

I'm not sure how, but Jake's confidence is contagious. So, I put my hands up innocently and let him handle it, the bumps and jolts in the road making the ride feels more like an adventure than a casual drive.

After about ten more minutes on the dirt trail and me getting increasingly curious, the trees open up. Suddenly, we're right next to this wide, shimmering river. The winter sunlight bounces off the water in a way that makes it look like the surface is covered in diamonds. The trees along the riverbank are tall. I feel like we've stepped out of time, into some hidden paradise no one else knows about.

As we drive down the narrow dirt trail, the trees become denser, their tall trunks casting long shadows in the late afternoon sun. After a while, Jake turns down a narrow drive way right next to the river. At the end of the drive way is a small clearing and in front of us stands a beautiful cabin made entirely of pinewood. It's simple yet stunning, like something out of a postcard. The rich, honey-colored wood seems to glow in the diffused light, and the porch has two wooden chairs facing out toward the forest, looking as peaceful as you could get.

Jake pulls the car to a stop and turns to me, a small smile tugging at the corner of his mouth.

"Well, here we are," he says casually, like this isn't the most picturesque spot I've ever seen.

I get out of the car, staring up at the cabin, completely taken aback. "This place is incredible, Jake. Is it yours?"

Jake nods, stepping out to join me in the wintery tundra. "Yeah. Bought it a while back."

I raise an eyebrow, still staring at the cabin. "I didn't know you had a place like this. Why didn't you ever mention it before?"

He shifts his weight slightly, his tone relaxing as he looks up at the cabin. "Well… it's not something I talk about much. I got it when I was going through some stuff. You know… when things were rough at home with my parents."

I glance at him, hearing the shift in his voice, the way it drops a little when he mentions his past. Jake doesn't talk much about the rough patches in his life, I can only imagine what he means. With a sick mom and a dad who didn't accept Jake for who he was, there were times when his own house, his life, must've felt more like an anchor than a home.

I want to ask more, to dig deeper, however, I can feel the weight of the conversation settling in. Instead, I try to lighten the mood. "So… you throw big parties here with all your friends, right? A secret cabin in the woods sounds like the perfect spot."

Jake laughs quietly, shaking his head. "Not exactly. No one knows about this place. Not Tess, not Brody… no one."

I blink, surprised. "Wait—no one?"

Jake shrugs, his eyes scanning the cabin, like he's seeing it again for the first time. "Nope. This place is just for me. It's my getaway, you know? When things get too loud or too crazy, I come here. It's like a safe haven. Somewhere I can just… breathe."

I look at him, realizing the depth of what he's saying. Jake, who's always so composed in front of everyone else, has this hidden place—his retreat from the world. Now he's sharing it with me.

"So, why bring me here?" I ask quietly, the question slipping out before I can stop myself.

Jake's smile is softer now, more thoughtful. "I don't know. I guess I wanted to share it with someone. You've been there for me through so much and I thought you'd understand why this place matters to me."

I feel my heartbeat through my chest at his words. Jake doesn't open up easily and the fact that he's sharing this part of himself with me—it means more than I can put into words.

I smile, trying to keep things light even though I feel the importance of the moment. "Well, I'm honored to be the chosen one. So… are we going inside, or are we just gonna stand out here staring at your very fancy cabin?"

Jake chuckles, walking toward the porch and motioning for me to follow. "Come on. I'll show you around."

As I step into the cabin, it becomes clear that this isn't just Jake's hideaway—it's his safe space. The walls are filled with paintings, sketches, and random art pieces, some half-finished, others complete. It's not the kind of place you'd call "well-decorated," except that's the beauty of it. This is where Jake's mind runs free, without the pressure of impressing anyone or sticking to deadlines. It feels raw, unfiltered—like the purest version of him.

The place is a bit of a mess, honestly—paintbrushes scattered everywhere, a canvas leaned up against a wall with streaks of red and blue still drying, old coffee mugs piled on a side table. Except it doesn't feel chaotic. It feels like a sanctuary, a space where time stops and nothing matters except the art.

As I scan the room something by the window catches my eye. A small table with two cups of instant noodles, a kettle, and a single candle right in the middle. It's such an odd, unexpected setup that I find myself staring at it for a second. I look at the noodles, then at Jake, and back at the noodles.

"When did you set all of this up?" I ask, genuinely wondering when Jake would've had the time to do all of this.

"Honestly," Jake says, lowering his head and rubbing the back of his neck. "I came out here this morning and set this up, planning on asking you to come to lunch with me and just hoping you'd say yes."

"Did you really think I'd say no?" I smile. "Something you should know about me, I will never say 'no' to carbs."

A moment of silence passes between us.

Then, out of nowhere, we both burst out laughing.

I mean, it starts small—just a chuckle—then it spirals out of control. Jake's laugh is contagious, this deep, hearty sound that makes my own laughter build up until I can't hold it in. I fall back, collapsing onto the wooden floor, clutching my stomach as I laugh harder than I have in weeks. I can barely breathe and my cheeks are starting to hurt from smiling so much.

I glance over at Jake, who's curled up in the corner, wiping tears from his eyes. He's laughing so hard he can barely stay upright, his shoulders shaking as he tries to catch his breath.

"What... what even is this setup, Jake?" I finally manage to gasp between laughs, pointing toward the noodles and the candle like it's some kind of bizarre art installation.

Jake wipes his face, still giggling as he shakes his head. "I have no idea. I just grabbed whatever I had in the pantry, and… well, this is what we ended up with."

I push myself up onto my elbows, still laughing. "So, the grand feast for today is instant noodles by candlelight? Classy."

Jake snorts, throwing a nearby cushion at me. "Hey, I didn't say it was going to be fancy. Come on, you can't deny the candle adds a nice touch."

I catch the cushion and toss it back at him. "Oh, for sure. Nothing says 'gourmet' like instant noodles and a single candle at a cabin in the woods."

Jake leans back against the wall, wiping the last of his tears away. "Honestly, I wasn't planning much and then I realized I didn't have anything over-the-top for us to eat. So… here we are. It's still better than nothing, right?"

I grin, finally catching my breath. "Jake, it's perfect. In the weirdest way possible, but still perfect."

After a couple of minutes, Jake finally gets up, shaking his head in disbelief at our little laughing fit. His stomach makes an unexpected growl, loud enough for both of us to hear it. "Alright, alright. Let's eat before these noodles get cold. Not that they can get any worse than they already are," he says, walking over to the table and grabbing the kettle.

LOVE & FROST

I push myself off the floor and join him at the table, still chuckling under my breath. Jake fills the cups with hot water from the kettle, then sets the chairs. The whole setup is ridiculous, yet somehow it feels right. This moment, in the middle of nowhere, with nothing except instant noodles and a candle, is exactly what we both want.

I need this more than I've ever needed anything, even air. I've never felt a connection like this, not even with Daniel. Looking back now, I see that I was fooling myself, pretending I was happy. The truth is, I was more afraid of being alone than anything else. Now I understand—being with someone you don't truly love is far lonelier than being by yourself.

As we sit down and start eating, the only thing I can do is shake my head. "I don't think I've ever had a more quirky meal with someone."

Jake grins, slurping up some noodles. "Yeah, but you'll remember this forever. Who else can say they've had candlelit instant noodles in a secret cabin?"

I laugh, taking a bite. "You've got a point. This is definitely a first."

The conversation flows easily after that. We start off talking about the exhibition, how the final day is going and the people who have shown up. Jake shares a few stories about some of the clients he's been dealing with, which have me laughing all over again.

"Okay, so this one guy," Jake says, waving his chopsticks in the air as he speaks, "comes up to me and says, 'I want something bold, something that screams art,' and I'm thinking, 'Dude, what does that even mean?'"

I nearly choke on my noodles, laughing. "Wait, he actually said that? Screams art?"

Jake nods, grinning. "Yup. Dead serious. So, I just show him the loudest piece I have, all reds and blacks and he loves it. I mean, come on. Screams art? What kind of direction is that?"

"Sounds like he has no idea what he's talking about," I say, still giggling. "I mean, hey, as long as he's buying, right?"

"Exactly," Jake replies, shrugging. "At the end of the day, if he's happy, I'm not complaining."

We keep talking, the conversation bouncing from one random topic to another—art, music, the weirdest things we've eaten, and everything in between. It's easy, comfortable, a nice break away from all of the exhibition stress, before all the chaos. Just me and Jake, laughing, talking, and eating terrible noodles.

At one point, I look over at him, catching him mid-laugh and something about the moment makes my chest tighten. Here we are, in this ridiculous, perfect little cabin, laughing like idiots over noodles and it hits me how much I missed connection like this. Jake isn't just my friend or the guy I've been helping out with the exhibition. He's more than that.

Jake and I walk side by side along the riverbank, the sound of our boots crunching in the snow. The sun dips lower in the sky, its warm orange hues spilling across the river, painting everything in shades of amber and gold. The reflection dances on the water's surface, making the river look as if it's flowing with liquid light. The crisp winter air bites at my cheeks, but it feels refreshing after the heat of the cabin and our makeshift lunch.

I find peace in the soft rush of the river as it flows over smooth rocks. It's quiet—serene, almost like the world has slowed down just for us. The stillness of the moment settles over me, bringing a sense of peace I didn't realize I needed until now. The trees lining the bank stand tall and bare, their branches etched like silhouettes against the luminous sky, while the snow-covered ground stretches before us like a fluffy, white blanket.

Jake walks with his hands shoved in his pockets, his breath coming out in warm puffs that rise into the cold air. I can feel the comfortable silence between us, the kind that only exists when you're truly at ease with someone. No pressure, no need for words—just the calmness of the moment, the quiet companionship, and the sound of the river as it carries everything downstream. It feels like we've stepped out of the rush of life and into our own little world.

The cold nips at my skin, but I barely notice it. The weight of everything—the exhibition, the chaos of the past few days—seems to melt away with each step we take. For the first time in what feels like forever, there are no distractions, no responsibilities.

As we talk more about the exhibition and it's success, Jake casually reaches for my hand, lacing his fingers through mine. I feel a small jolt in my chest that I ignore, because I'm not pulling away.

Jake glances at the river, gesturing toward a spot near the bank. "You see that little bend over there? It's a great spot to catch trout. I've spent a few afternoons out here, just casting a line and letting the world disappear."

I look where he's pointing, trying to imagine Jake out here, fishing by himself in the middle of nowhere. "You're telling me you actually fish? Like… with a pole and everything?"

Jake smirks. "What, you don't think I can fish?"

I chuckle. "I just never pictured you as the outdoorsy type. You're usually so busy with your art."

Jake squeezes my hand lightly. "Yeah, well, you'd be surprised what you learn to do when you need a break from people. It's peaceful out here. Just me, the river, and the fish."

I nod, understanding that more than he probably knows. "I get that. It's nice out here. Everything's quieter."

He smiles, his eyes glancing toward the woods that surround us. "Exactly. There's a lot of stories about this place too, you know. The locals talk about it like it's got history. Legends, even."

I raise an eyebrow, intrigued. "Legends? What kind of legends?"

Jake grins, that mischievous look flashing in his eyes. "Well, for one, there's the famous story about the Chupacabra and Wendigo fighting over territory right where the cabin stands."

I blink, staring at him in disbelief. "Wait—what?"

Jake chuckles, clearly enjoying himself. "Yup. According to the locals, there was this epic battle between the two. Chupacabra, you know, the creepy goat-sucker creature, and Wendigo, the man-eating spirit from Native American folklore. Apparently, this land was prime real estate for their spooky activities."

I feel a slight chill run down my spine, but I try to play it off. "That's… a lot. So you're telling me I've been hanging out where two legendary monsters duked it out?"

Jake laughs, pulling me a little closer as we walk. "Hey, it's just a story. Probably meant to scare the kids around here. If the Wendigo does come for us, don't worry—I'll protect you."

I snort, trying to hide my nervousness behind a laugh. "Oh, thank God. I was getting worried for a second. It's good to know I have a hero by my side."

Jake grins, nudging me playfully with his shoulder. "Of course. All those years of head-banging in football are finally gonna pay off when I'm out here fighting off mythical creatures."

I laugh, feeling the tension in my chest ease up. "That's comforting. I'm not sure how good your high school football skills are against supernatural creatures, but I'll take it."

Jake shrugs, his smile widening. "You'd be surprised. I've still got some moves."

I shake my head, smiling at the ridiculousness of it all. The whole idea of a Chupacabra and Wendigo brawl is insane, somehow, Jake makes it sound less terrifying and more like an adventure we'd face together. That's the thing about him—no matter what the situation, he always makes me feel like I'm safe. Like I'm not alone.

We keep walking, our hands still intertwined, as Jake points out different spots along the river where he's fished or explored. The conversation flows easily, moving from silly legends to random stories from our pasts. It's the kind of wandering, aimless conversation you can only have with someone you're completely comfortable with.

Jake finally asks a question I've been waiting for someone to ask, "So, have you considered moving back to Everest?"

I let out a small chuckle, trying to think of the easiest answer to give. "I mean, not really. I just have so much going on back in New York, but maybe someday."

"Yeah, I get that." Jake lets out a delicate breath.

After about two hours of walking and talking, the sun has dipped lower, casting long shadows across the trees. I glance around, realizing how far we've gone. "I think we've wandered pretty far. Maybe we should head back before it gets dark."

Jake looks around, nodding. "Yeah, you're right. Don't want to be out here when the Wendigo decides to show up."

I laugh, shaking my head. "Right. I'm trusting you to keep me safe."

Jake grins, giving my hand a light squeeze. "Always."

seventeen

Tess' New Year's Eve party kicks off around 10 in the evening and I find myself standing just outside High Peak, taking a deep breath before walking in. It's only a five-minute walk from the exhibition, but it feels like a world away from the turbulence and anxiety of the recent days. The party is intimate, with about 30 to 35 people showing up, honestly, that makes it better. It's more personal, more laid-back. After everything we've been through, this smaller crowd feels like a much-needed break.

When I step inside, the café is filled with ambient lighting and the DJ plays a mix of Christmas music and hits from the last year. It's enough to set the tone without overwhelming anyone. It's perfect, really. The music blends with the low hum of conversations, creating an atmosphere that makes you want to relax and let everything go for a while.

I spot a few familiar faces right away. Some of the artists who showed their work at the exhibition are clustered in small groups, laughing, chatting about their own upcoming projects. One corner of the room even has a small setup where a couple of artists have started painting—right there at the party. I can't help smiling at that. They can't stop creating, even when they're supposed to unwind.

As I make my way toward the refreshment table, I hear snippets of conversation floating through the air.

"So, I've been thinking about hosting my own exhibition," one artist says, his voice full of excitement. "I mean, after seeing how well Jake's went, why not?"

"I've got some pieces that are almost ready," another artist chimes in. "I just need to find the right space. Maybe next year. Who knows?"

Hearing that makes me feel a small swell of pride. Jake's exhibition is clearly inspiring more than just the attendees. It's starting to ripple through the art community and people are already thinking about what they can do next.

I reach the bar and order an espresso martini, nothing fancy, but enough to keep me awake until midnight. As I take a sip, I glance around the room, appreciating how different this feels from the frantic energy of the exhibition. Here, it's calm. People are in their own world, talking about art, sharing ideas, and just being in the moment.

"Nice turnout, huh?" I turn and see Maria standing beside me, holding a drink of her own. She looks more relaxed than she has all week, her usual seriousness replaced with a lightness I haven't seen in a while.

"Yeah, it's pretty great," I reply, smiling. "I didn't expect it to be so... chill."

Maria nods, taking a sip from her glass. "That's the vibe Tess wanted for tonight. Nothing too crazy, just a chance to unwind and let the dust settle. I think after all the events of this last weekend, we needed this."

I chuckle, glancing at the small group of artists still painting in the corner. "Do you think they will ever stop working?"

Maria follows my gaze and laughs faintly. "I doubt it. That's what happens when you love what you do, I guess."

"Fair enough," I say, nodding. "It's kind of cool, though. Seeing people just... create, even when they're supposed to be relaxing."

Maria smirks, looking at me sideways. "You should join them. I know you've been itching to do something creative."

I roll my eyes, though I can't deny the itch is there after watching Jake all week. "Yeah, maybe another time. Tonight, I'm just enjoying the peace and *almost* quiet."

Maria shifts uncomfortably, her hands wrapped around her coffee cup as she glances at me with an almost apologetic expression. "Hey, I feel like I need to tell you something," she says quietly, her voice barely audible over the chatter of the café. "I never actually liked Jake."

I blink, taken aback. "What?" I twist in my seat to face her fully, locking eyes with her. "What do you mean?"

Maria sighs, taking a deep breath before continuing. "Ethan, I went to school with your sister, Jamie. We've been close for a long time. And, well... she told me shortly after you arrived that she thought you liked Jake. She said you might need a little push."

I furrow my brow, trying to process her words. "Wait, so you never had feelings for Jake and you told me you did because... what? You thought that would make me run to him and confess my feelings?"

Maria opens and closes her mouth a few times, like she's searching for the right way to explain herself. "It wasn't exactly like that," she finally says, her voice gentle, but firm. "I wasn't trying to manipulate you, Ethan. I just wanted to help. I could see how much you cared about him. I also saw how much you were holding back. I thought if I said something, if I... put the idea of competition in your head, it might give you the push you needed to take a risk and tell him how you feel."

I stare at her for a moment, my mind racing as I try to make sense of it all. "So, all this time... you were just trying to get me to see what I already knew deep down?"

Maria nods, her expression relaxing. "Yeah, exactly. I'm sorry if it was confusing or if it hurt you in any way. That was never my intention. I just wanted to remind you that sometimes, if you really want something—or someone—you have to be brave enough to go after it."

I sit back in my chair, letting her words sink in. There's a part of me that feels a little foolish for not seeing it sooner, there's also a strange sense of relief. Maria wasn't a threat; she was trying to help me realize what I've been too afraid to admit to myself.

"I get it," I say after a pause, giving her a small smile. "Honestly, I probably needed that push. I've been so caught up in my own head, worrying about what might go wrong, that I didn't even think about what could go right."

Maria smiles, a genuine tenderness in her eyes. "Exactly. Sometimes we just need a little nudge to take the leap."

I look over at Jamie in the corner, watching us with a knowing grin and shake my head with a laugh. "I should've known she was involved."

Maria chuckles, glancing at Jamie too. "Yeah, she's a bit of a mastermind when it comes to these things. She only did it because she cares about you—and so do I.

You and Jake... you two are good together. Anyone can see that."

I nod, feeling a mix of gratitude and relief. "Thanks, Maria. I appreciate you being honest with me—and for giving me that push, even if I didn't realize I needed it."

Maria reaches across the table and gives my hand a reassuring squeeze. "You're welcome, Ethan. Also, I wanted to ask if you'd ever consider partnering up with me as a marketing consultant?"

"What do you mean?" I ask.

"You would partner with me and we would work with my clients together, you'd be able to connect them to the right people. You can set your own prices and charge what you're worth, I'm telling you, these artists want nothing more than to make it big, so they'd sell their soul to have you on board." Maria smiles.

"But I live in New York," I choke up a little, thinking of all the possibilities this could open for me and moving back home.

"Just think about it," Maria smiles.

I return the smile, feeling lighter than I have in days. "I will. Thanks again, Maria. Really."

She gives me a wink. "Anytime. Now go get your guy."

The party picks up, but it's just as relaxed as Jake had promised. I stand with Tess and Brody, drink in hand, chatting about everything under the sun. Tess is in the middle of a chaotic road trip story when I glance over at the corner of the room. There, at a small table, Maria and Jamie are deep in conversation.

"Tess, look at Maria and my sister," I say, nodding toward them. "Do you think there's something going on there? Because from what I'm seeing, it honestly looks like they're about to start sucking on each other's tongues."

Tess glances over and chuckles. "Oh great, just what we need—those two joining forces. Imagine the trouble they could stir up."

Brody grins, raising his drink in a mock toast. "To the dynamic duo, Maria and Jamie. Plotting world domination, no doubt."

I laugh, but there's a knot in my stomach. I have a feeling I know exactly what they're talking about. Ever since Jamie showed up earlier, she's been giving me these knowing looks and now, with Maria involved, I can only imagine the subject of their conversation.

"I bet they're talking about you and Jake," Tess says casually, reading my mind.

I blink, caught off guard. "Wait—what?"

Tess smirks, clearly enjoying my reaction. "Oh come on, Ethan. You didn't think you could keep your little situation with Jake a secret, did you?"

Brody raises an eyebrow, leaning in. "Yeah, dude. Everyone's been noticing. The way you two are always together, how you look at each other. It's not exactly subtle."

I feel the heat rising in my face. "It's not like that. We aren't anything serious, I don't think. Does everyone forget that I'm going back to the city soon."

Tess snorts, taking a sip of her drink. "Sure, just friends. I'm pretty sure Maria and Jamie are over there plotting how to push you two together."

"I doubt that," I laugh sarcastically.

I glance over at them again. Jamie catches my eye and, instead of looking embarrassed, she grins at me, giving a little wave. Maria, noticing the interaction, leans in and whispers something to Jamie and they both laugh.

"Great," I mutter, looking down at my drink. "My sister's discussing my love life with Maria. That's exactly what I need."

Brody chuckles, nudging me with his elbow. "Hey, they're just rooting for you. Honestly, everyone kind of is."

I shoot him a look. "What's that supposed to mean?"

Tess grins, taking a bit too much satisfaction from this. "Come on, Ethan. We're just saying… maybe it's more than just friendship."

I sigh, rubbing the back of my neck. "It's not that simple, okay? We're close, yeah, it's just, you know... complicated."

Tess leans in, raising an eyebrow. "Complicated, huh? So, there is something more going on."

Before I can respond, Brody raises his glass, grinning. "Well, whatever it is, you two are great together. Whether you want to admit it or not."

I roll my eyes, though I can't stop the small smile tugging at my lips. "You guys are relentless."

Tess smirks. "We just want to see you happy, Ethan. From where we're standing, Jake makes you happy."

I glance across the room again, watching Maria and Jamie laugh, clearly enjoying their little inside conversation. Part of me wants to march over there and tell them to stop meddling, and another part of me is kind of grateful.

My phone buzzes in my pocket, pulling me out of the conversation. I pull it out and see a text from Jake.

Jake:

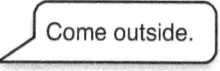

Come outside.

I smile, glancing around the room. Jake was mingling with the guests earlier, keeping everyone entertained, but I haven't seen him in a while. Without saying anything to Tess or Brody, I slip my phone back into my pocket and casually make my way toward the exit.

"Hurry back! It's almost midnight!" Tess shouts.

Stepping outside, the cool night air hits me, a refreshing change from the heat of the party. The moon hangs high in the sky, casting a mellow light over the parking lot and there, leaning against the side of the building, is Jake. He looks relaxed, but a little worn out, his hands shoved into the pockets of his jacket.

"Hey," I say, walking up to him. "You good? What's up?"

Jake smiles, except it's the kind of tired smile that tells me he needs a break. "I had to sneak out. The party's great and all, I just needed to get some air, away from all the questions and the 'how did you do it?' talk."

I chuckle, leaning against the wall next to him. "Yeah, I get that. It's been non-stop for you."

He glances over at me, that devious flicker back in his eyes. "Figured I'd steal you away, too. I knew if I stayed in there any longer, they'd rope me into another conversation about art theory."

I laugh, shaking my head. "Yeah, you definitely looked like you needed an escape plan."

Jake pushes off the wall, nodding toward the moonlit street. "Wanna take a walk? Get away from all the noise?"

I don't need any convincing. "Sure, let's go."

We start walking, the sounds of the party fading behind us. The silence between us is comfortable, a break from the constant chatter inside. After a few minutes, I glance over at him.

"So," I begin, breaking the quiet, "how'd the meeting with Senator Alfort go? I didn't get a chance to ask you about it earlier."

Jake's face lights up and I can see the thrill in his eyes, even in the dim light. "It went really well, actually. He had a lot of good things to say about my work, which was kind of surreal. I mean, the guy's a senator. He could've just been polite, but he seemed genuinely impressed."

I smile, feeling a surge of pride for him. "That's amazing, Jake. I knew he'd like your stuff."

"Yeah," Jake nods, "he even mentioned the possibility of commissioning something in the future."

I stop in my tracks for a second, staring at him. "Wait, what? Commissioning your work?"

Jake grins, clearly enjoying my reaction. "Yeah. He said he's got some spaces in his office that could use something bold and modern. It's not a sure thing, yet it's still pretty wild to think about."

"Jake, that's huge!" I say, unable to hide my excitement. "Do you realize how big that is? A senator commissioning your art? That could open so many doors."

He shrugs, though I can see he's trying to stay humble. "I don't want to get ahead of myself, but yeah, it's pretty big. Even just hearing him talk about it made everything feel worth it."

I shake my head, still processing the news. "You're going places. This is just the beginning."

Jake laughs tenderly, his voice more relaxed now. "I hope so. I mean, it's been a crazy few days, getting that kind of recognition feels like a huge step forward."

As we walk, Jake tells me more about the night. He's met a few big clients—people from the art world who were impressed with his exhibition and hinted at future collaborations. It's all stuff he should be celebrating inside the party, but here he is, sharing it with me instead.

"And then there was this gallery owner from Chicago," Jake says, shaking his head. "He said he'd keep an eye on my work, maybe even showcase it in the future. Honestly, it's all happening so fast, I don't know how to process it."

I grin, nudging him with my shoulder. "Chicago? That's awesome! It's all because you're good at what you do. This is what you've been working toward for years. You deserve all of this."

Jake glances at me, his expression easing. "Thanks, Ethan. That means a lot."

With the moonlight guiding our way, the calm of the night wrapping around us. It's peaceful out here, away from the noise and the questions. Just Jake and I, walking and talking like I've always wanted. As he talks about his recent successes, about the senator who's shown interest in his work and the gallery owners who want to meet him, there's something more layered into the moment. The way he shares it with me like I'm the only person who really understands what this all means to him, makes everything feel... bigger.

It's not just about his success. It's about trust. He's letting me in, opening up about his hopes, his fears, the pressure that comes with his growing recognition. There's a quiet vulnerability in the way he confides in me and I realize that this isn't just any ordinary conversation. This is him pulling back the curtain, showing me a part of himself that not everyone gets to see.

It feels like we're standing on the edge of something important, like this moment could be the foundation for something even deeper between us. His words, his gestures—they're all laced with a significance that I can't quite explain, I just can feel it. It's like the air around us has thickened, charged with an unspoken understanding that there's more to us than just friendship, more to this moment than just a casual walk under the stars.

The weight of everything he's telling me, the way he looks at me when he speaks—it all makes my heart race. I feel it in my chest, this undeniable sense that we're crossing an invisible line, moving toward something real, something we've both been circling around for a while now.

It's terrifying, but it's also exhilarating. This is what I've been waiting for—Jake, sharing his life with me in a way that feels raw and intimate. It's so much more because this isn't just about his career anymore. It's about us, and how we fit into each other's worlds. The night, the soundless world around us, the way our footsteps sync as we walk—it all feels like a prelude to something I've been too afraid to name until now.

This moment feels bigger because it's not just about where Jake is headed in his career—it's about where we could be headed together.

After a while, Jake chuckles. "You know, I was worried you'd be stuck inside all night, getting grilled by Tess and Brody."

I laugh, shaking my head. "Oh, they were definitely grilling me. Something about how everyone's talking about you and I."

Jake raises an eyebrow, smirking. "Oh yeah? What are they saying?"

I shrug, trying to play it cool. "Just about how close we are, how we're always together. You know how people love to talk."

Jake doesn't say anything for a moment. Instead he just looks at me, his expression unreadable. Then he smiles. "Well, maybe they're right."

I feel my heart skip a beat as I keep walking, letting the moment settle around us.

We're walking in the chill of the moonlight, our fingers laced together like it's the most natural thing in the world. The air is cool and crisp, the kind of night that makes you feel like time is slowing down. Everything about the evening feels right. As we stroll, Jake turns to me, his voice faint but curious.

"So, what did you think of my paintings?" he asks, glancing over at me with those familiar bright eyes.

I smile, glancing at him sideways. "I loved them, Jake. I always knew you were talented, I mean, before it was football and now it's art. Seeing all of your work together like that… It felt like I could see a part of you in every piece. It's hard to explain, but it was incredible. I really enjoyed the whole exhibition."

Jake blushes a little, the corners of his mouth lifting into that playful grin that always gets to me. "You're just saying that because we're friends."

I shake my head, squeezing his hand a little tighter. "No, seriously. I mean it. You put yourself out there in a way most people can't. That's brave. For what it's worth, I think your work is amazing."

He chuckles subtly, but I can tell my words hit home. "Thanks, Ethan. That means a lot coming from you."

For a while, the conversation drifts into a more personal territory. We talk about random memories from years ago, our fears, dreams, things we haven't really said out loud before. I feel the heat rising to my face every time Jake smiles at me and I can't stop my heart from racing. Every word seems to carry a weight that wasn't there before and even though we're laughing and teasing each other, there's something more to it, something that lies beneath the surface.

Suddenly, in the middle of a sentence, Jake stops walking. I feel his hand gently tug mine, pulling me to a stop with him. I turn to face him, the world falling quiet around us. His face is serious, but his eyes have a spark —something I haven't seen before.

"Ethan," he begins, his voice low, almost nervous, "I... I like you."

The words hit me like a brick. For a second, I'm not sure I've heard him right. My heart starts pounding in my chest, so loud I'm sure he can hear it. I open my mouth to say something, but nothing comes out. I just stare at him, my mind racing, my body frozen in place.

Jake doesn't move. He just watches me, his eyes searching mine. Then, without saying anything, he reaches up and places his hand gently over my chest. His fingers rest right where my heart is hammering against my ribs and I can feel the warmth of his touch through my shirt. The contact sends electricity through my body, making everything else around us blur into nothing.

"I can feel your heart pounding," Jake whispers, his thumb gently brushing against my chest. "What are you feeling right now, Ethan?"

I'm completely at a loss for words. My mind is spinning, trying to process everything, but all I can focus on is the way his hand feels on my chest, the way his eyes are locked on mine. My throat goes dry and for a moment all I can do is take shallow, uneven breaths that seem too loud in the silence around us.

Jake's face is so close, his breath hot against my skin. My pulse is racing, and I can feel every beat hammering under his hand. I don't know how to respond. I don't know what to say. I only know what I feel.

Without thinking, I reach up and grab his hand that's resting over my heart and pull him closer. Our bodies are barely inches apart now and I can see the slight flush on his cheeks, the nerves in his eyes. But there's no going back from this. Not anymore.

In the distance, church bells chime, signaling midnight. Signaling the New Year.

I swallow hard, my voice barely above a whisper. "Jake... I..." But I can't finish the sentence. Instead I lean forward, closing the space between us in an instant. My lips crash against his and everything else—every doubt, every question—disappears. It's like the world has gone still, like the only thing that exists is the feeling of Jake's lips against mine.

The kiss is electric. Passionate. Desperate. His hand tightens over my chest, fingers curling into the fabric of my shirt, as if he needs to hold onto something solid. My hands find their way to the back of his neck, pulling him even closer, deepening the kiss until there's nothing between us except heat and the rhythm of our hearts.

Jake responds immediately, his other hand sliding up to my waist, gripping me tightly as if he can't bear to let go. His lips are soft, but demanding, matching the intensity of the moment. It isn't just a kiss—it's everything we haven't said, every glance, every touch that's led up to this. I feel his breath hitch as our mouths move together, hungry and unrestrained, the kind of kiss that makes you forget who you are, where you are.

I can feel the heat of his skin, his chest pressed against mine, his heart beating just as wildly as my own.

Every touch, every shift of his body against mine makes me feel alive in a way I hadn't expected. It's overwhelming, in the best possible way.

After what feels like an eternity, but also not nearly long enough, we pull back, our breaths heavy and uneven, sending billows of fog up toward the stars, our foreheads resting against each other's. I keep my hands on the back of his neck, my fingers brushing against his skin as we both catch our breath.

Jake's eyes are still closed, his lips slightly parted and I can feel the faint tremble in his hands as they rest on my waist. When he finally opens his eyes, there's a softness there I haven't seen before. Something vulnerable and real.

"Ethan," he whispers, his voice barely audible, "I've wanted to do that for so long."

I smile, my heart still racing in my chest. "Me too, Jake. Me too."

I wake up slowly, the early morning light filtering in through the window. It takes me a second to remember where I am. The fragrant scent of Jake's cologne lingers on the sheets and when I shift slightly, I realize I'm not in my own bed. I blink a few times, my mind catching up, then it hits me: I'm at Jake's studio.

I stretch out, feeling the comfort of the bed around me, the sheets velvety and smelling like him. The faint flutter of excitement from last night is still humming in my chest. The memory of our kiss flashes in my mind and I can't help but smile to myself. Everything about last night feels surreal, like it hasn't fully sunk in yet.

I glance around the room, half-expecting to see Jake lying next to me, except he's not there. The room is empty, but I hear quiet sounds coming from outside the door. I push the covers back and sit up, running a hand through my hair. The space has this comforting feel—inviting, lived-in, like it has a piece of Jake in every corner.

I get out of bed, pull on my shirt from last night ,and head toward the door. As I step into the hallway the smell of coffee hits me and I follow it into the small kitchen. There he is—Jake—standing by the counter, casually pouring coffee into two mugs, looking as relaxed as ever. His bare back is to me and A smile creeps across my face at the sight of him.

"Morning," I say, my voice still a little groggy.

Jake turns around, grinning when he sees me. "Morning. Sleep okay?"

I nod, stepping closer and leaning against the counter. "Yeah. Your bed's pretty comfortable."

He chuckles, handing me a mug of coffee. "Good to know. Figured you could use this."

I take the mug from him, the heat of it seeping into my hands. "Thanks. You always make the best coffee."

Jake shrugs, a playful smirk on his lips. "I try."

We move over to the couch and sit down, the morning quiet settling around us. It feels strangely normal, like waking up together is something we've done a hundred times before. I take a sip of the coffee and glance at him, trying to gauge where his head is at after everything that happened last night.

"So," I begin, swirling the coffee in my mug, "about last night…"

Jake raises an eyebrow, his lips twitching into a small smile. "You mean the part where we kissed, or the part where you passed out on my bed?"

I laugh, feeling the heat rise to my face. "Both, I guess."

Jake leans back on the couch, his eyes gentle. "Last night was… a lot. In a good way."

I nod, taking another sip of my coffee. "Yeah, it was. I wasn't expecting everything to happen the way it did, but I'm glad it did."

Jake smiles, his gaze dropping to his coffee for a moment. "Me too, Ethan. I've wanted to tell you how I feel for a while now, I just wasn't sure if it was the right time… or if you felt the same."

I set my mug down on the coffee table, turning to face him fully. "I do. I mean, I don't know where this is going, however, I do know that I want to find out."

Jake's eyes meet mine and, for a second, we just sit there, the silence between us comfortable and reassuring. He smiles a comforting, genuine smile that makes my heart flip all over again.

"Good," he says quietly. "Because I want that too."

Before I can say anything else, my phone buzzes in my pocket, snapping me out of the moment. I pull it out and glance at the screen, my eyes widening when I see the number of unread messages.

"Uh, give me a second," I say, swiping through the notifications. "Looks like Jamie's been trying to reach me all morning."

Jake smirks, leaning back on the couch. "I figured she might start wondering where you were."

I open one of Jamie's messages and it's just a stream of texts. I can't help but chuckle as I scroll through them.

Jamie:

???

Jamie:

Where are you???

Jamie:

Are you alive?

"She's freaking out," I mutter, then hit the call button. The phone rings a few times before Jamie picks up.

"Ethan!" she says immediately, her voice full of concern. "Where the hell are you? You disappeared last night and you didn't text me back."

I glance at Jake, who's watching me with that amused look on his face. "I'm fine, Jamie. I'm with Jake. I, uh, spent the night here."

There's a moment of silence on the other end of the line and I can almost hear her brain processing what I've just said.

"With Jake?" Jamie finally repeats, her voice dropping in tone.

I clear my throat, trying to play it cool. "Yeah, I... stayed over. We talked last night and we both told each other the truth, that we like each other. It's no big deal."

Another pause. Then, out of nowhere, Jamie giggles. The kind of giggle that makes you want to hang up immediately.

"Oh my God," she says, her voice teasing now. "Did you two—oh no, wait, don't answer that! I don't need the details. Seriously, Ethan, finally. I've been waiting for this."

I roll my eyes, glancing at Jake, who's clearly trying not to laugh at the one-sided conversation he's overhearing. "Okay, okay, relax. Nothing crazy happened. We just... talked."

Jamie giggles again, clearly not buying it. "Uh-huh. Sure. Talked. Well, don't let me interrupt whatever's happening now. Enjoy your little morning-after with your boyfriend. I'll talk to you later."

Before I can respond, she hangs up. I stare at the phone for a second, then sigh while putting it back in my pocket.

"Well?" Jake asks, grinning at me. "What'd she say?"

"She was… excited, I guess," I say, shaking my head. "She definitely thinks more happened than what actually did."

Jake chuckles, setting his coffee down and leaning a little closer to me. "So… nothing crazy happened, huh?"

I feel my heart skip a beat again, his closeness making it hard to focus. "I mean, not yet."

As we sit on Jake's couch, sipping coffee and letting the morning sink in, I can tell something is weighing on him. His usual easy smile fades, replaced by a look of uncertainty. He sets his mug back down and turns to me, his voice lower than usual.

"Ethan, there's something I've been thinking about since yesterday," he says, his eyes meeting mine.

I frown, already feeling the knot in my stomach tighten. "What's going on?"

He hesitates for a second, like he's not sure how to start. "It's about… you being here. I mean, you've got a good job in the city, a whole life there. So I've been wondering… how long are you planning to stay here? When are you going back?"

I blink, taken off guard. I haven't even thought about it, not seriously. Everything has been moving so fast—coming back to town, helping with Jake's exhibition, last night—it all feels like a blur. I don't have any concrete plans. The thought of leaving hadn't really crossed my mind too much up until now. I wasn't planning on getting into anything serious. That said, one thing is for certain, I'm serious about Jake. The weight of it hits me like a ton of bricks.

"I… I don't know," I admit, my voice quieter than I expect. "I wasn't planning on staying long when I first came back. My job's in the city. That's where my life is— or at least, where it was."

Jake nods, but there's something in his expression that tells me he's been expecting this. "Yeah, I figured. I get it—you've got responsibilities there and your career. I don't want to get in the way of any of that. I just… I guess I've been thinking about what happens next. Between us."

His words hang in the air and I feel my heart twist in my chest. *What happens next*? We haven't had time to talk about it. It's all so new, so fragile and now I feel this pressure, like I have to make some kind of decision. And the truth is, I think Jake has been right all along. This is my home. It always will be.

"I don't want to leave," I start, my voice shaky, "my job... my whole life is back in the city. That's what I've worked for. That's where my career is, my apartment, everything I've built. Now..."

I trail off, my thoughts all tangled up. Being back in my hometown, with Jake, feels like a different kind of life. One I haven't expected to want. Is that enough to change everything? Is that enough to make me stay?

Jake must notice the conflict in my eyes because he reaches out, resting a hand on my knee. "Ethan, you don't have to decide right now. I just wanted to talk about it. I don't want you to feel like you have to stay because of me."

"I don't feel pressured," I reply quickly, though the truth is, I'm not sure what I feel. "It's just... complicated. I didn't expect to be in this position and now everything's so up in the air."

Jake nods, his thumb gently rubbing my knee. "I know. I get that this is a lot to process. I just want you to know that I'm here. Whether you decide to go back to the city or stay, I'll support whatever you choose."

I let out a long breath, leaning back into the couch. "I don't know what I'm supposed to do. Part of me thinks I should go back. I worked hard to build my life there and I can't just walk away from it. Then... being here, with my friends, my family, with you, it feels like maybe there's something for me here that I didn't realize before."

Jake's eyes soften, but he doesn't push. "You're torn."

"Yeah," I admit, running a hand through my hair. "I'm completely torn."

We sit in silence for a few moments, the weight of the conversation settling between us. I don't know what the right answer is. I don't know if I can just walk away from my life in the city, I also don't know if I can walk away from Jake.

"I wish it were easier," I mutter, more to myself than to him.

Jake gives a small, understanding smile. "Big decisions never are. Whatever you decide, you won't be making it alone. I'll be here, Ethan, whether you're living in the city or five minutes down the road."

I look at him, the uncertainty in my chest still heavy, yet his words make it feel a little lighter. "Thanks, Jake. I don't have all the answers yet, although knowing you're okay with whatever happens… that helps, a lot."

He squeezes my knee gently, his smile reassuring. "Take your time. I'm not going anywhere."

nineteen

When I walk into my parent's house, it's quiet because Mom and Dad are both at my grandparents house, like they do every New Year's Day. The only sound is the low hum of the fridge and the occasional creak of the floorboards. Jamie is lounging on the couch, flipping through a magazine. She looks up when I enter, her eyes lighting up immediately.

"Well, well, well, look who decided to show up," she teases, tossing the magazine aside. "How was your night?"

I hesitate for a second, not sure where to start. "It was… good. Actually, I need to talk to you about something."

Jamie raises an eyebrow, sitting up straighter. "Oh, this sounds serious. Is it about Jake?"

I blink, surprised she already knows. "Uh, yeah, actually."

Before I can even finish the sentence, Jamie squeals and jumps off the couch, throwing her hands in the air like she's just won the lottery. She bounces around, her excitement practically radiating off her.

"I love being right! I knew the moment he came to our house with a present that you two had something going on," she says, clapping her hands. "Oh my God, I'm so happy for you!"

I stare at her, completely bewildered. "Okay, hold on. Why are you acting like this is some big revelation?"

Jamie plops back onto the couch, grinning from ear to ear. "Well, Maria and I had a little bet going."

"A bet?" I ask, raising an eyebrow.

"Yup," Jamie says, practically glowing. "I told Maria that you and Jake would end up together within a week. She thought it would take at least a month, so now she owes me fifty bucks." She winks, clearly proud of herself.

I can't help but laugh. "You made a bet on my love life? Really?"

Jamie shrugs, completely unbothered. "Of course I did. I mean, come on, it was so obvious you two were going to end up together. I just didn't know it would take you twelve years to figure it out."

I shake my head, grinning despite myself. "You're unbelievable. My life's not a betting race, you know."

"Sure it is and I just won," she shoots back, beaming. "Okay, seriously, what did you want to talk about?"

Her tone shifts and she leans forward, her expression soothing. I sigh and sit down next to her, suddenly feeling the weight of what I have to say.

"It's about the city," I begin slowly. "I'm supposed to go back soon. My job, my whole life is there. But... now, with Jake... I don't know. I don't want to mess things up by leaving, on the other hand I also don't know if I can just walk away from everything I've built over there."

Jamie listens quietly, her eyes fixed on me, then asks, "So, what are you saying? You're thinking of leaving Jake behind?"

I shake my head quickly. "No. I don't want to. It feels like I'm stuck between two worlds. I have this career, this job I've worked hard for and then there's Jake. I can't just stay here without figuring out what to do."

Jamie crosses her arms, watching me for a moment before she asks the question I'm not ready for. "What's more important to you, Ethan—your job or Jake?"

I freeze. Her words hit harder than I expected and I feel my chest tighten as I think about it. "Jake," I say quietly, almost automatically. "Jake's more important. But," I pause.

"But, what?" Jamie asks, leaning in closer.

"Maria said she'd like me to work with her as a marketing consultant with her clients," I shrug.

Jamie smiles gently, like she's been waiting for me to say it. "Then there's nothing to think about. Stay here, Ethan. You have a job here. Life's too short to spend it worrying about a career if it means losing someone who actually makes you happy."

I let out a breath I didn't even know I'd been holding, the weight of her words settling over me. "What if I regret it? What if I can't find a job here? Or what if… I don't know, what if it doesn't work out between Jake and I? I can't just throw everything away."

Jamie gives me a gentle, knowing look. "You're not throwing anything away. You're choosing what makes you happy. Even if things get complicated, you'll figure it out. You always do. But you can't live your life afraid of what might happen. You have to make choices based on what you want right now."

I stare at her, feeling a mix of relief and anxiety all at once. "What if I make the wrong choice?"

"What if you don't?" she asks firmly. "Because you're not basing this on fear. You're basing it on love. And if Jake makes you happy, then that's worth more than some job in the city."

I swallow hard, nodding slowly. "Yeah. It is."

Jamie leans back, crossing her arms with a satisfied smile, eyes flicking briefly down to her phone. "Oh. My. God," she says, each word emphasized with delight. "Have you checked Instagram?"

I glance at her, one eyebrow raised. "No... why?"

"Because Jake just posted a photo," she says, a teasing edge to her voice.

Curiosity piqued, I reach for Jamie's phone. As soon as I see Jake's Instagram handle, 'j.collins.art,' my heart skips a beat. I tap on the post and my breath hitches when the image fills the screen.

It's a photo of Jake and me from last night, walking down Main Street. We're holding hands, our smiles soft and unguarded, like the world had fallen away, leaving just the two of us in that moment. Whoever snapped the picture captured something raw, something that goes further than I thought anyone could see. I scan the scene again, knowing this wasn't a random capture. Someone close to us must've taken this—one of the friends who've been not-so-subtly pushing us together since I got back to Everest. My mind immediately goes to the four usual suspects.

I feel my mouth hang open and the comfort of something more than just surprise spreads through my chest, settling deep in my gut. A swell of emotions surges through me—hope, gratitude, fear, and this overwhelming sense of belonging, all tangled together. I almost forget Jamie's sitting right there, watching me.

"Eth," Jamie prompts gently. "You good?"

I don't look up at her right away. My eyes are still fixed on the image, on the unspoken connection it so clearly shows. It feels like looking at something I've longed for, but never fully acknowledged—until now. My hand tightens on the phone and finally, I lift my gaze, a smile tugging at the corners of my lips. However, this smile feels different. It's unguarded, unburdened.

"No," I say, my voice tender, almost in awe of the weight of what I'm feeling. "I'm not just good. I'm fucking great."

I glance back down at the photo and it hits me— these last ten days, being home, being with Jake, everything that's felt so uncertain for so long, suddenly feels clear. There's a peace in my chest that I haven't felt in years, like all the scattered pieces of my life have finally fallen into place.

The joy of being here with him, the sense of comfort and ease I've rediscovered in his presence—it feels like something bigger than I can name. It feels like home. It's not Everest, not this town, not even the familiarity of old routines. It's Jake. It's him beside me that makes everything feel right, like I belong here with him, in this moment, in a way I haven't belonged anywhere else in a long time.

Jamie's voice cuts through my thoughts. "Eth, I know you. In that photo, you look genuinely happy. Happier than I ever saw you with Daniel."

I meet her eyes and for the first time, I don't feel the need to guard my feelings or hide behind half-truths. I nod slowly, my smile growing, a wave of certainty settling over me.

"I was," I admit, the truth finally sinking in fully. "I am. I'm happier than I've been in a long time."

I know it's not just a passing feeling. It's not the fleeting rush of something new or exciting. It's a quiet, steady kind of happiness—one that feels earned, one that feels real.

"Good. Then you know what you need to do. Stay here, be with Jake and find a way to make it work. It's not going to be easy, but nothing worth having ever is."

I let out a nervous laugh. "You make it sound so easy."

Jamie laughs, giving me a playful nudge. "It's not easy, but it's worth it. Besides, you know Mom and Dad will love having you back home. Plus, I'll be here to help. So will Maria. And Jake... well, you know he'll support you."

I look at her, feeling a sense of clarity I haven't had before. "Thanks, Jamie. I needed that."

She grins, throwing her arm around my shoulders. "Of course. Now, go tell Jake that you're staying. And make sure Maria coughs up my fifty dollars."

I laugh, shaking my head. "I still can't believe you bet on this."

"Hey, a girl's gotta make some extra cash," Jamie teases, giving me a wink. "Now go be happy, Ethan. You deserve it."

epilogue

ONE YEAR LATER

The snow is falling delicately outside, covering the small town right outside of Chicago, in a perfect layer of white. I stand by the window of the little cabin Jake and I have rented for the weekend, watching the snowflakes drift lazily down while strumming some random chords on the ukulele Jake gave me last year. Everything looks peaceful, like the world has decided to slow down just for us.

"Hey, you're going to freeze standing next to the open window like that," Jake's voice comes from behind me, comforting and familiar.

I turn, smiling as he walks over and wraps his arms around my waist. He rests his chin on my shoulder and we stand there for a moment, just watching the snowfall together. It's hard to believe that a whole year has passed since I made the decision to stay in this town, since I chose him.

"I was just thinking about how different things are now compared to last year," I say softly, leaning back into his warmth.

Jake chuckles, pressing a kiss to the side of my neck. "Yeah? Good different, I hope?"

I smile, feeling the familiar flutter in my chest that always comes when he's close. "Definitely a good different."

He turns me around to face him, his hands resting on my hips. "Hard to believe it's already been a year, huh? Feels like it flew by."

"Yeah," I agree, my eyes meeting his. "At the same time, it feels like we've been together forever."

Jake grins, that playful glint in his eyes. "Well, you're stuck with me now, so I hope you're not tired of it yet."

I laugh, wrapping my arms around his neck. "Not even close. In fact, I was thinking we could make this whole 'first anniversary' thing a tradition. We'll come back here every year."

Jake raises an eyebrow, his smile widening. "Every year? You're sure you won't get bored of this little cabin?"

F. A. SENG

I glance around the cozy space—the fire crackling in the hearth, the smell of pine and cinnamon in the air. It's perfect. "Nope. Not even a little. Besides, there's something magical about spending winter out here. The snow, the quiet… it's like our own little world."

Jake's smile eases and he pulls me in a little closer. "Yeah, it does feel like that, doesn't it?"

We stand there for another moment, just holding each other, the warmth of the fire surrounding us. I can't help but think back to how uncertain I was a year ago, how torn I felt between my job in the city and staying here with Jake. Now, standing in this cabin with him, I know I made the right choice.

"Remember how I once told you that my sister asked me what was more important—my job or you?" I say, my voice quiet.

Jake chuckles, his hands gently rubbing my back. "Yeah, I remember. I didn't know what you'd choose back then."

I smile, pressing my forehead against his. "I did. I chose you. I will always choose you"

Jake's expression softens, his eyes locking with mine. "I don't think I would've made it through this year without you by my side."

My heart swells and I kiss him gently, feeling the usual butterflies spread through me. After everything we've been through, every challenge we've faced—

starting a new job in town, building a life here together—
it feels like we're stronger than ever.

"Speaking of making it through," Jake says, pulling
back slightly, "you've handled the Michigan winters
pretty well. I thought you'd be crying for the city after
your first snowstorm."

I laugh, rolling my eyes. "Listen, New York gets
snow too. Also, did you forget that I was born and raised
in Everest?"

Jake smirks, leaning in to kiss me again.

I kiss him back, slow and sensual.

He laughs, pulling me tighter into his arms. "You
know, I'm really proud of us. We made it through a lot
this year. Moving in together, starting new routines,
figuring out how to share a space without killing each
other over the dishes."

"Hey," I say, grinning, "I'm still working on the
dishes thing, alright?"

Jake laughs, pressing a kiss to my forehead. "I
know. I'll keep letting it slide because you make a mean
cup of coffee."

I roll my eyes, though a smile still tugs at my lips.
"Guess I'll keep making coffee, then."

We settle onto the couch, the fire crackling beside
us as we sit together under a blanket. I rest my head on
his shoulder, feeling the rise and fall of his chest as he
holds me close. There's something so peaceful, so right,

about this moment. It's everything I wanted when I made the decision to stay in Everest—to be with Jake.

"Here's to many more winters together," I murmur, feeling the weight of the year lift as we sit there, side by side.

Jake kisses the top of my head, his voice kind and low. "Many more winters, many more anniversaries, and whatever else life throws at us."

"And more *Mean Girls* nights?" I laugh.

"Of course," Jake smiles. "Always more of those."

We stay like that, wrapped in each other, watching the snow fall outside the window. For the first time in a long time, I feel completely at peace. Because this is home—Jake is home. I know, without a doubt, that whatever comes next, we'll face it together.

"Happy anniversary, my love," Jake whispers, his breath warm against my ear.

"Happy anniversary," I whisper back, smiling as I close my eyes, ready for whatever the future holds for us.

In this quaint cabin, *"You Belong with Me (Taylor's Version)"* playing softly in the background, I know that this—right here—is just the beginning of our story.

Acknowledgements

The journey of writing *Love & Frost* has been an incredible adventure, filled with moments of inspiration, late-night writing sessions, and the unwavering support of those around me. As I look back on this journey, there are a few special people who have made this book possible and to whom I owe a deep debt of gratitude.

First and foremost, I want to extend my heartfelt thanks to my editor, Lauren. Your keen eye for detail, your insightful feedback, and your patience throughout the editing process have been invaluable. You've helped shape this book into something I am truly proud of, and for that, I am eternally grateful.

To my Alpha Reader, Ashley, thank you for being the first set of eyes on this story. Your early feedback, honest insights, and encouragement gave me the confidence to keep pushing forward. You've been a critical part of shaping *Love & Frost*, and I'm so grateful for your time and dedication.

To my "baddies with the saddies," you know who you are. Your support, humor, and love have been my lifeline. You've been there through the highs and lows, providing both encouragement and a much-needed reality check. Your friendship means the world to me, and this book would not have been possible without your unwavering support and love.

And finally, to my partner, Jason. Your constant belief in me and my work has been my anchor. Your love, patience, and understanding have been a source of strength. You've celebrated my successes and lifted me up during the tough times. Thank you for being my rock and my inspiration. This book is as much yours as it is mine.

To all of you, I extend my deepest gratitude. *Love & Frost* is a testament to your love, support, and encouragement. Thank you for believing in me and my story.

With love and appreciation,
F. A. Seng

MORE BY F. A. SENG

The 'Greylith' Series
Greylith

Stand-Alone Romances
Love & Frost

F. A. Seng is a versatile author known for his fantastic worlds and now he's crossing genres. Following the success of 'Greylith', he is excited to venture into the realm of LGBTQIA+ romance with "Love & Frost." This heartfelt story explores themes of love, identity, and self-discovery, showcasing F. A. Seng's dedication to inclusive and diverse storytelling. Passionate about representing different voices and experiences, F. A. Seng continues to captivate readers with his genuine and powerful narratives. In his spare time, F.A. Seng loves to explore the intersections of fantasy and reality, always finding new ways to inspire and connect through his writing.

.